MW00940027

The Twilight Overlord

Kyle Tianshi

Book Series

The Twilight Overlord

The Eternal Flame

The Endless Abyss

ACKNOWLEDGMENTS

I spent most of my summertime in 5th grade writing this book series. With great appreciation, I am very lucky to have helpful and ingenious parents, who gave me so much encouragement and support throughout the long journey of writing every day. My beloved sister, Emily often brought me ice cream and chips to my room in the middle of my writing time. She was always so excited to hear I added another 50 pages to my story in one day. My mom also introduced me to Jim Fanshier, who kindly guided me through the process of editing and publishing which seemed easy but quite tedious. There are many other people who have quietly supported me: my grandparents who believed that I was the greatest writer in the world; Peter Fellingham and his parents who were the first few readers for my books and provided me with their valuable feedback; my friend Leanne who read through my story with great enthusiasm; and my favorite dog, Nimbus who slept next to me for most of my writing.

ISBN-13: 978-1981617494
Printed in the United States of America
First Printing, 2017

For Mom

The Twilight Overload

Chapter 1

My whole school year has been very odd and creepy. Every day, when I walked back home to my small apartment in the gloomy streets of Los Angeles, I always felt like someone was stalking me. Looking around, I saw in the shadows of the alleys a dark, hooded figure. Sometimes the guy had two horns on its head. I told my mom about it, and she took a deep breath and said, "You're just imagining things, William. Don't think about it." And what was weird was that she never usually called me William unless I was in trouble or needed to know something important.

We once went on a field trip to an aquarium last year, in sixth grade. I was hoping that this time, I wouldn't accidentally do something bad. And just saying, I always do something bad. We were looking at some sharks swimming in a pool of water below us when I got myself in trouble.

Suddenly, a shiver ran down my spine. I jumped. Everyone thought I was crazy, except for Zach, my best friend.

He's awesome, but sometimes a bit creepy (and also very clumsy). And his appearance doesn't help either. He looks like a gangster, with ripped jeans and messy black hair like me.

Except that my hair is actually black when his hair seems to have a greenish tint. His eyes are also green, which is completely not the color of mine.

My eyes, at first, seem to be dark brown, but when I look in my mirror and examine them closely, they seem to be a rainbow of colors. My mom says that the mirror just isn't good, but I didn't believe her one bit. Now my mother is the best mom in the world, but I can't just believe everything she says all the time.

And you might be wondering where my dad went. Apparently, my mom and dad got married, and then my dad had to go on an adventure. He left before my mom had me, and he never came back.

"Something is wrong," I muttered while we gazed at sharks swimming in endless circles. "Just something."

"It sure is," Zach answered. He dropped his pencil on the ground and bent to pick it up.

When we were watching the alligators crawl around in their sandy pit and taking notes on what they were doing (sleeping), I felt as if we were being watched once again.

I turned around and scanned the area. Suddenly, I saw the scary hooded figure. I screamed and scared my teacher and the students so bad that some of them dropped their books into the alligator pit. I guess we weren't retrieving those. (It was sort of funny anyway, but don't tell anyone, okay?).

I apologized and said that I got frightened, but no one believed me anyway. So I was suspended for a week for "attempting to frighten people" and "screaming".

During my suspension, Zach came to my house every day after school to do his homework with me. I thought that the reason was that his parents were going to come home late that week and it was just a weird coincidence.

But, that most likely wasn't the case.

Then, on our last day of seventh grade, I really messed up. We were going on a field trip to a retirement home. I already got in trouble when we were going home in a bus. The class bully, Rufus (that's the name of Zach's dog, I think), was pestering my best friend Zach by tossing chip crumbs into his lap.

"He is so… annoying. Can I just tell him to stop?" I growled.

"Don't, Will. You'll get in trouble again."

"Still." Finally, we arrived at the retirement place. It looked like any old apartment building in Los Angeles, about ten stories high, but there was a park right next to the building. Dark, ominous clouds loomed in the horizon.

We headed out to the yard, and we were supposed to play some sort of game with them. I decided to try to play catch, but I ended throwing the ball right into my teacher, Mrs. Key's, face.

So I had to sit down as a timeout. As I looked around, I saw a man wearing an orange coat and an orange tie. He was wearing sunglasses, which was really odd because it looked like it was about to rain. His hair was dyed orange-red, like a bunch of burning flames. He was looking at us from outside of the park with his hands crossed. A shiver ran down my spine. I wondered what he was doing, probably nothing but still, I felt uneasy. I turned back to watch Zach fumble with the ball and trip over his feet.

We took the bus back to school, and then things started to go really wrong.
It was almost time for dismissal, so we packed our bags and got ready to leave. I felt very accomplished because I lasted the whole school year without getting into too much trouble.

"Stay after class, William," Mrs. Key said. "I need to talk to you." Again, I don't exactly like being called William. I hadn't told anyone to call me my real name. We walked out into the hallway.

"You know you shouldn't be here."

"What?"

"You will never get to Fort Azari. Zachary was foolish to try to protect you." I still had no idea what she was talking about.

"What... what do you mean...?" I backed up into a wall. She stepped closer. I looked onto the breezeway and out to the courtyard to see if anyone was around.

"I should bring you to Yharon, but I wouldn't want to. I'm really hungry, and I'm sorry, honey..." Her hands turned into claws, and her teeth turned into fangs. Her skin was wrinkly and old. I instantly lowered my head because I didn't want to see how her face looked.

Suddenly, out of nowhere, Zach appeared. He was holding some kind of wooden stick with green lights coming out of it.

"Stop!"

"No!" Mrs. Key screamed. She bared her fangs at him. I wondered why Mrs. Key would be so scared of a person who drops his lunchbox on a regular basis.

"Don't hurt my friend!" he demanded. Just out of impulsiveness, I picked up a rock and tried to throw it at the demon Mrs. Key.

"Oh well, honey. I'll just blow him into smithereens!" She turned yellow, then orange, then red. It looked like she was going to blow up. If it weren't for Zach, who leaped forward, tripped, and pushed me out of the way right before she did explode, I would have been toast.

There was a huge explosion, and Zach and I got blown back. I conked my head against a wall and sat there for a bit with my eyes closed. When I opened my eyes, there was a huge smoking crater where Mrs. Key was.

"What...was that?" I murmured. My head still throbbed with pain. Kids started rushing through the hallway, looking for the source of the sound. In the end, the principal said that I wanted to take some money from Zach, and that we got into a fight. Zach beat me up, but I managed to explode an oil tank that was in his backpack.

I mean, c'mon! There's no way that we would have gotten into a fight. We were best friends but I got expelled. Dang it.

I still knew that there was something wrong with Zach and Mrs. Key, but I couldn't figure it out.

Then, I would have to wonder where my new school would be. Little did I know, it was in the middle of the woods.

After school, Zach came back home with me. I kept bugging him about what happened after school, but he just acted as if nothing happened. And if he was faking it, he was a really good actor. We walked to the cluster of apartments where I lived. I tromped up the stairs to my home dejectedly, and I heard Zach muttering behind me. "Gotta get him to camp." I wondered what he was talking about. Probably some video game. He dropped his lunch bag back down the stairs and went back to pick it up.

I opened the door and called, "Mom, I'm home."

"Okay, honey! I'm in the bathroom right now. Is Zach with you?"

"Yeah. But why does he need to be with me?"

I set my backpack down on the ground, and I sank into a couch in the small apartment in Los Angeles. I gazed out the window. There was the same man I saw at the retirement home wearing an orange coat standing at the bottom of the apartments. He wasn't wearing sunglasses this time, and his eyes looked like balls of heat, and he emitted a fiery glow. Just as I looked out, the man raised his hands and the sky started to turn gray, and then purple. Suddenly, two massive blue, translucent worms came out from the clouds that were now raining and thundering.

"Zach!" I called. "Zach! Am I imagining things, or…"

"Where? Where?" He looked out the window. "Oh no! Where's your mom, Will?" Zach asked frantically over the thundering.

"What are those things?" I yelled, and I tried to run back. But I tripped over Zach's feet and ended up on the ground. Luckily, my mom came out from the bathroom.

Zach told her to go to the car, and we sprinted down the seven flights of stairs in our apartment and rushed into the sedan. The spectral blue worms changed their course and started charging right toward the car. My mom revved the engine up, and we drove away.

Then Zach started to do some pretty weird and spectacular things. He seemingly disappeared (although he turned into a fly) and suddenly, a bear appeared on the road. It roared at the worms and then turned into a cheetah and sprinted back to the sedan.

"Those are storm weavers," Zach told me gravely. "And I think they were sent down by Yharon..." and his voice trailed off because when he said Yharon, the storm weavers immediately sped up and almost smashed into the sedan. My mom suddenly swerved and avoided them.

"How'd... what was the bear and everything? How'd you turn into all those things? And what are storm weavers? What are you're saying right now?"

"I'll tell you later! Now's not the time! I need to protect you right now!"

"Protect me? Why would I need protection?" I said. Then I looked at his face and saw that I hurt his feelings. "Sorry. I'm real impulsive sometimes."

My mom kept on driving like a madman while Zach settled down and gave her directions to someplace.

The land in front of us turned gray, old, and corroded. The boulders all around us were slowly flaking away, and even the sturdy concrete of the road that we were on was going away at the touch of the tires. There were ravines all around us that extended all the way down to nothing.

"What is this place?" I inquired. "Are we-"

"Now's not the time, dear!" my mom squeaked.

When we entered the new landscape, the storm weavers became even faster, and started firing blue lasers at us. The sedan groaned as a blast collided with the back of the car.

"Uh oh," I said nervously.

"What?"

I think there's a ravine that stretches across the road..." There definitely was.

"There's another one?" Zach was talking about the ravine. "That means the Corruption is spreading even more now."

"What's the Corruption?"

Then, many corroding monsters floated out of the gaping stretch of the ravine. They looked like flying scorpions, with razor sharp fangs poking from either side of their mouths. Their bodies all were dripping pieces and reforming as quick as possible. They rained a trail of rotten, disgusting chunks wherever they went, which was, unfortunately, straight toward us.

"Not corruptors!" Zach groaned.

They started to shoot vile globs of spit from their mouths, so my mom suddenly stopped, which was a horrible idea.

A storm weaver smashed right into the trunk of the sedan (which was already half obliterated by the laser beam) while the other cosmic worms flew right alongside firing lasers. We were flying diagonally toward the sky at the speed of a rocket. All the windows shattered and the only response was;"Ahhhhhhhh!" from all of us (maybe it was only me, but, what's the difference?).

Zach changed shaped again into a llama, was it? and he started to fire spitballs at the storm weavers. At the touch of the spit, the worms started disintegrating into a bunch of blue clouds.

"WHAT?" I screamed, the wind whipping in my face.

"They're prone to animal's spit!" Zach yelled as another storm weaver smashed into the car.

We went flying so fast that the last storm weaver couldn't even catch up to us.

In front of us, the corroded land stopped, and rolling grassy hills were spread out in front of us. There was a big lake with forests, where I saw a big one-story wooden cabin. Right next to it, there was a big open pavilion area also made out of wood. On the right of the woods, a frozen tundra with a frost encrusted lake stood. Behind that, there were a few smoking mountains. I saw a cloud floating in the sky, and there seemed to be a castle type thing on it. What? I thought. There were many cabins and buildings dotted along the land, and a large wall stretched around the whole thing.

But, I didn't have time to enjoy the scene.

The car was spinning in circles while we were still screaming. The storm weaver smashed into an invisible wall and it spun around and flew back to the clouds. We almost splashed down into the lake when a girl ran out from the biggest house surrounding the lake.

"Randy!" she called.

She moved her hands, and the wind somehow blew us down slowly. We settled down into the grass groaning and she ran over.

The person who saved us was a pretty girl that had flowing shoulder-length, brown hair and appeared to be about the same age as me. She had twinkling blue eyes that reminded me of the sky and wore a white shirt that said *Fort Azari* and blue jeans.

"Are you okay?" she asked us, helping us get out of the car. Other people started coming out of the buildings to see what was happening.

"Yeah, maybe," Zach said. "Stupid…" He kicked a chunk of the wreckage away and hurt his big toe.

"Gosh Zach! Are you okay? Are any of you okay?" she asked, looking at us. I rubbed my head, which already had a dent in it from a few hours before, thanks to Mrs. Key.

She turned to me. "This is Fort Azari, and I'm Selena. This will probably be your home for the next few months, so you better get settled here." Then she turned to Zach and whispered, "Is he the one?" Zach nodded nervously. Then she said out loud, "Thank goodness you're here, because Zach isn't a very good protector-"

"Hey!" he protested.

"Just kidding, but what's your name?"

"William, but I don't like being called William. Just call me Will."

"Okay, Will. Now let's go."

…

A few hours later, My mom and I were in the house that Selena had come from, the Meeting House, they called it. In it, there was another tall man inside the house who appeared to be the leader of them all. He had rumpled brown hair and had pale blue eyes that, for some reason, seemed to have a fiery glint in them. He seemed to be in his thirties. Sitting next to him, Zach fiddled with a rubber band and kept looking around nervously.

"Is he the one?" the blond man questioned.

"Yeah. At least we think so," Selena responded. I had so many questions swarming in my head that I couldn't even think.

"Wait," I said. "What's all about this "is he the one"? Are you talking about me?"

"Well," the tall man said. "A few weeks before, I had visions about a demigod with Zach. And I saw in my vision that he would save this place."

"Save the fort from what?" Now, that I had a chance to butt in, my stream of questions just kept coming. "Who's Yharon? How did the storm weavers get here? Who are you, anyway?"

"My name's Randy. I'm an Overseer," he said. "Which means that I can see into the future, sort of like a prophecy. Here we go..." He stiffened up, and his eyes turned pure black.

"You must enter the land of nightmares," he murmured in a rasping voice that was not his. "You..." He gasped and toppled back into a chair.

"That was short," Selena grunted. "He's supposed to tell us what will happen. But he didn't give much information this time." I, personally, was totally creeped out and was glad that he didn't continue talking.

My mom had kept quiet the whole time but finally, she burst out. "Was he talking about Will?"

"Well," Zach said. "There's the Corruption you see out there right? Well, it's spreading and soon it will reach our magical borders."

"And the borders won't withstand the Corruption." Selena added.

"Well, then. Fix your borders!" I exclaimed.

"All the corruption spreading is the work of Abaddon and Yharon," Zach told, ignoring me.

"Who's Yharon in the first place?" I asked.

"Yharon's the man that summoned the storm weavers, remember?" Zach said.

"Well," I thought about it for a moment. "We got away from him pretty easy, right? And how are these people real in the first place?"

"That was only a bit of his power. If you see him in real battle mode, you'll see what I'm talking about. And also, he's under an even more powerful enemy, Oblivion. If we ever live this long to see him, it's not gonna be good."

"So, where is this Oblivion?"

"Trapped in a box. But, about the Corruption." Selena interrupted. "We can hold off the Corruption for a bit with our purification powder, but our supplies are running low and we will run out of powder soon. The only other way is to stop Abbadon."

"Who's Abbadon? I heard you talking about him earlier."

"Oh," Selena said. "He's the Lord of Shadows, and if we stop him, the Corruption will withdraw."

"Why? And how are these people real?"

"Because he's the Twilight Overlord and darkness! What did you expect?" I shrugged and said, "I hoped that he was the god of rainbows and unicorns or something like that. Then all would be happy."

"And we have about a month until the powder runs out," Zach told me. "But for now, let's not worry about that and let's give you a tour around."

…

Selena led me up a gravel path into the woods; where there was a nice wooden cabin nestled in the thick shrubbery. There were vines creeping around the building, and small windows were on the sides.

"This is the cabin for the Grovites. They can do woodland magic, like growing thorns to tangle someone, or summon protective shields of wood, or other things. All people like Zach are from this cabin." Selena said.

"But how do you get your powers?"

"Well," Selena said, "Everyone is just born like that. A god or goddess marries a human, and they have a demigod child."

"So, how many other gods are there?" This was already getting way too complicated in my head.

"So the gods. There are two major gods. Reality. He holds the fabric of reality in his hands, and his children... well... he hates them."

"Why?"

"Nothing. There's Galaxius. He can control all of the elements, so he's sort of like an all-powerful guy. So then there's the less major gods who still are really powerful Aquaia. She controls all of the water."

"Wait," I interrupted. "So she can control all the water that's in my body right now?"

"Duh, no. That would be weird. I'm a descendant of Aer, she controls the air. Finally,

Aphelion is the god of fire. There are a few other minor gods, but I really don't want to name-"

"Who are they?"

"Shut up, please-"

"No."

"Everyone here has some person in their family who relates all the way back to Reality, Galaxius, Aer, Aphelion, and Aquaia, or, their parent is a god. But it's rarer to be a child of a god or goddess. They're usually a lot more powerful than normal demigods.

"Are you a daughter of Aer? Sorry. Just curious."

"I am."

"Then how do the Grovites get their powers?"

"Sometimes, the parents have something related to the power. For instance, Zach's mother was a biologist.

"Then what am I?"

"We don't know yet. We'll need to test you, to see if you can do anything useful."

"Useful? What do you mean-"

"So," Selena interrupted, "The leader of the Grovites is called Allen. He's in there, probably. Anyway, let's move on."

"But why can't we go in?"

"Come on! I'm on a tight schedule, okay?"

"Okay then." "He's just a friend of mine. Anyway," Selena continued. "The fiery guys, the

Aphelists, live in the big fiery mountain past this place. They're really good at blacksmithing, but… oh! It's getting pretty late now, so, I guess I'll take you back. You've been through enough for today. You'll sleep in the Meeting House, and I hope you know how to get there. I'll meet you there."

…

Dinner was great at the Meeting House. Some people like Selena and others went outside to enjoy the sunset, but I decided to eat in the Meeting House. The food was a delicious chicken barbecue. Afterward, Randy announced that there was a newcomer to Fort Azari. One person called out: "What type is he?" I figured that he was talking about my parent.

"We don't know yet," Randy answered. There was much groaning and muttering among the people. Luckily, some people weren't too bummed, and I met a few nice people.

Connor Li was a tall Asian boy from the cabin in the woods with a friendly smile and a deep voice. He seemed a bit older than me and was really upbeat. Even though he was really nice, I always felt like he had some kind of joke or trick ready to pull out from behind his back.

Finally, I went back into the Meeting House and prepared for sleep. Randy pulled me over for a bit.

"Don't worry about anything. We'll be fine. The first day is always the worst."

"Okay," I said, but I felt like he was comforting himself more than me.

Over the next few weeks, I fell into a routine that I got really used to. We first all gathered together to eat breakfast. Then, we all scattered off to our activities.

First, I went to try out blacksmithing. This blond guy called Yohan helped me. He had shaggy yellow hair and glowing orange eyes like balls of fire. I looked at his hands and saw that they were calloused and showed many marks.

I ended up breaking the hammer I was using, and Yohan said that I would get better. But we weren't listening, since we were all too busy cracking up.

Then, some people tried to make me cast some woodland magic. I tried really hard, and I actually made some poison ivy grow and gave Allen a rash.

"So I guess you're a Grovite," Allen said. "You'll probably move here unless you're a… never mind. It's not possible."

"You're a what?"

"It's nothing." I thought in my mind, *why does no one answer my questions?*

Then, Selena brought me over to the icy area. There was a large, barren cabin covered with frost and snow that stood next to the frozen lake that

I had seen on my crash-landing. She knocked on the door and it was opened by a tall and gruff girl wearing a heavy, white parka.

"What do you want, Selena?" she demanded.

"We have Will here, Nina. You know. That guy. Can you see if he can do any ice magic?"

"The newbie, huh?"

"Hey!" I exclaimed. "I'm not a newbie!"

"You wanna go, huh? Because I don't think you can beat me in a battle." I did not want to get into a fight with her. Selena interfered before the talk could get more heated up. "Can you just test him, please? I want to get this over with." I could tell that Selena didn't like Nina either but had to put up with her.

"Fat chance that he'll be it, but I'll do it," Nina grumbled. She took me over to the frozen lake. "Summon some icicles for me please."

"What?"

"I said summon some icicles."

"But how?"

"Just... think. Think like how you summoned that woodland magic. C'mon!" She clapped her hands together like a soccer coach and glared at me.

And so I thought.

Suddenly, six rainbow daggers appeared all around me. A shockwave went through the ground and Nina and Selena fell down.

"Elemental daggers!" Selena gasped as she looked up from the ground.

I really didn't know what to do with the daggers, so I made them fire, and they smashed into the ground. There was huge elemental explosion of colors (I make great fireworks), and I was thrown back into the ground. The rainbow of colors cleared and in the place where the daggers had hit was a crater with blue shimmering crystals. In the middle, a knife made of the same blue crystals was lying with the blade stuck in the ground, just like King Arthur and Excalibur.

Nina and Selena gasped.

"Malachite!" Nina said.

"No way…" Selena murmured. Other people started coming out of the other cabins. I thought that I caused way too much trouble (and again, I had zero idea what any of them were talking about).

"Wow…"

"No way!"

"Who did it?"

"That's one of the legendary weapons!" Selena said.

"What's… what's a legendary weapon?" I asked. "And how did I do that anyway?'

"You're an elemental," Nina said. I felt like I should be honored, but Nina just gave me an evil eye like I was the worst thing since death. *And what's an elemental again?* I thought. *Sorry, but you people never tell me anything.*

"Take it out!" someone yelled.

I stepped forward and took hold of the dagger. It had a gleaming gold hilt, and the blade seemed to be made of pure blue malachite, hence the name.

"Can Will and I talk in private with Randy?" Selena spoke. "This is really important." Some people grumbled, but they let us go.

We walked back to the Meeting House with Randy and we sat down in the living room. There were four couches in the middle of the room on top of a red patterned rug. A table sat in the center of the rug, and some other tables and chairs were scattered around the place.

"First thing," Randy said. "Don't interrupt, because I've got a lot to say."

"Sure."

"Uh huh," Selena snorted sarcastically. "He's definitely going to listen here."

"Shut up," I growled.

"The Malachite is one of the two legendary weapons." Randy started. "The Malachite, combined with the other weapon, the Vesuvius, which is, unfortunately, in Yharon's palace, is thought to have the power to defeat Oblivion, but only if used correctly. Unfortunately, we're not exactly sure how to use it, or if it's even true. Either way, the two weapons are very, very powerful. The

Malachite first needs a cover made from the enchanted malachite in the crater back there that you made. If the blade strikes an object too hard, it… well… explodes. It unleashes pure energy that will obliterate any monster within a wide radius. And it'll probably obliterate any human too, but when you use it regularly like any sword, the blade will elongate to a three-foot sword. When you swing it, little blue sword projectiles will fire out and track your enemies. And, about being an elemental, well, very, very rare people are elementals. Actually, there hasn't been one in over a century. So you could be very powerful."

"Wait. How'd you get all this information in the first place anyway?"

"The legendary weapons were just myths, until now. So I'm guessing that everything about them is true."

"But, Malachite would probably break after me using it for a bit. I'm… well… not good at that stuff," I admitted. "Though not as clumsy as Zach sometimes."

"That I can believe," Selena joked.

"Now don't underestimate Zach. He might seem clumsy at first, but he can handle a sword pretty well. So, we'll use the malachite crystals all around it to make a casing." Randy said. "The crystals are very powerful, but not as powerful as the crystal used to make Malachite."

"Who made Malachite?" Just then, Nina stormed in.

"Thanks for blowing a hole in front of my cabin," she growled. And to make a point, she launched a few ice crystals at me. They should have been volatile, but a bit of elemental energy surged out of my body and shattered the knives.

"Sorry," I muttered, not sarcastically, but I guess Nina took it that way because she sent a full force blizzard of frost and ice at me and smashed me back into another table. Nina flew away - literally flew away - levitating on a plate of blue ice. Now I just made Nina even more of an enemy.

"She's a bit grumpy," Randy mumbled. "Always is. That's what you are when you're a Cryonite.

"What's a Cry-on..." I said.

"Oh," Randy answered. "They have control over frost and snow and ice. But, you can control almost anything, if you have practice. You saw how Selena controlled the wind to bring you down."

"By the way, you're welcome," Selena added. "I was expecting a thank you from you."

"Then where's her cabin?"

"In a cloud," Randy replied.

"What?"

"Yeah."

"Where?"

"Well, you might have seen it on your way in. You know. That cloud is always there. There's a cabin on top of it. Very nice view though, not so pretty in these hard times."

"Are there any water people?"

"Yes, but they are pretty rare," Randy replied. "I'm one, as a matter of fact. But I'm also… never mind." I'm still wondering how many secrets these people were keeping away from me.

"What about Zach?" I asked.

"He's a protector and a grovite. But, because you're an elemental, I have hope in you. I've been thinking about how to solve the Corruption problem, but we will need to summon Abaddon with the Key of Nightmares, which is in his fortress. Signus, his helper, might be following you, but we really have no idea. A quick hint, though. He's weaker in light, but very strong in shadows. That gives you an advantage."

"Why can't we just fight Abaddon there? I mean, you could ship all of the demigods there and..."

"He has way too much power in his castle. We'll need to set up defenses here. The Key of Nightmares is his most prized possession, which he can use to open a chest which contains Oblivion. He would do anything to get it back so-"

"How the heck did Oblivion get into a box?"

"Well, that's another story. But Abaddon and Yharon are almost prepared to unleash Oblivion."

"Fun," I said. "Well, let's get it over with. My mom probably won't allow me, though."

"Oh. Your mom is back at her apartment in Los Angeles."

"What?"

...

All credits go to Randy for sending my mom back home so I could go on an impossible quest. Thanks!

"Where do we go, anyway?"

"Well, Abaddon's fortress is in a part of the Corruption that's in New York. It's hovering on an island in the sky."

"A floating island?"

"Yes, dummy," Selena snorted.

"We have also crafted three cases for Malachite," Randy said. "More, just in case you break one. Good luck on your mission and be safe. We'll send you off tomorrow morning."

"But who's going with me? Am I going by myself, or..."

"Zach is going with you, and so am I," Selena said. "I haven't gone to the outside world since... never mind. I hope that this wasn't a wrong decision, going with you."

Later, Randy took me to my cabin, which was located right on the border between the forest and the snow. It seemed like any old room inside, with a bunk bed and a wooden table, plus some drawers and a bathroom.

I wish I had slept well, but I tossed and turned in my sleep. We had to sneak, which I wasn't especially good at, into a fortress and steal one of the most important objects in the world. I didn't think we could do it.

Finally, sleep took me.

...

I had a horrible nightmare. I saw Abaddon, sitting in his fortress, talking to someone else, probably Signus. Abaddon had two dark horns jutting out of his head. His face was cloaked, but I saw two purple eyes from underneath the hood. He had a purple and black chest plate with ancient runes carved on it. To his side, he held a perfectly black blade. On it were scenes of darkness and horrible pictures.

"Open the chest soon," he said.

"We should wait longer, sir. We need to get rid of the head. His power over water is too great. Also, that child, William. We need to get them to our side."

"Yes. We should."

"Go then, capture them. I will report to Yharon now." Then, my dream faded.

...

I was waken up by a very annoying mosquito. Then, it morphed back into Zach.

"Gah! What are you doing in here?" I exclaimed, and fell back in my covers.

"Sorry," he said. "We have to get up early. I'll leave now." He slowly backed up, fell over a bag on the ground, grunted, and left.

"This early?" I complained to myself. "Why?"

Ten minutes later I was dressed and ready for the trip. Zach had packed a bag with extra clothes, toiletries, and some money. Only Randy, Yohan, and Allen were up to send us off.

"Good luck," Yohan murmured. He patted my back.

"Thanks."

"You better get going," Randy said. "But first, your mom told me about your father."

"Well, yeah. I never really knew him. He was an explorer, and went everywhere. Once, he went on a journey to explore somewhere and never came back, right?"

"No. You-"

"Wait. So, my dad is Galaxius?"

"Yeah."

"So, he's not dead?"

"He's not dead. Most of the gods are in Aquaia's fortress underwater. Galaxia and Reality actually don't have any mansion or anything to stay in, but they're at Aer's palace."

"What's wrong with Aquaia's palace?"

"Nothing. You-"

"Why don't we go now?" Selena said who had been quietly waiting next to me. Surprising, she didn't say how stupid I must have been.

"Okay," Randy said. "We're going to go now. One of our older demigods will drive you to Las Vegas. That's as far as I can go."

"Let's go now," Zach said. Allen gave me a pat on the back and gave a goodbye huge to Selena. We loaded up in the van, and we zoomed away. I savored the look of Fort Azari. The Meeting House, the mountain looming in the background, the lush, leafy forest, the cloud hovering in the sky, even the icy plains, the frosty, cold, barren cabin and the small crater in front of it.

I saw someone else come out of the ice cabin. The person was very shadowy, and had a cloak wrapped around his or her head.

I held my breath.

The figure slowly worked the way into the forest. It appeared out the other side. He or she snuck up behind Randy, who was walking back to the Meeting House. Randy tensed. He whipped around and blasted the person with water. Suddenly, the figure lashed out and grabbed his throat. Randy dissolved into shadow. I gasped just as the van rounded a corner. The person looked straight at me.

I knew who he was. He was Signus, Abaddon's helper.

And now, Randy was gone.

Chapter 2

"I just saw Signus!"

"What?" the demigod said.

"He stole Randy!"

"What did he do, and what did he look like?" Selena asked.

"He had a black cloak wrapped around his body."

"That's Signus," Zach said.

"It looked like he choked Randy," I continued. "He grabbed his neck and he burst into shadow."

"That means he captured him," the demigod explained. "He might want to lure you to his castle. I'm not sure."

"But we need to go back for him!" I said. "We can't just leave him!"

"Unfortunately," he answered. "He'll be gone already. You need to focus on your mission." After that, we rode in deep silence, listening to the cars run by.

A few hours later, we arrived in Las Vegas.

"What do we do now?" I wondered.

"There's a bus that comes through." the demigod answered. "And we bought three tickets for you. It will take you to Denver in Colorado. Then, there's a train that takes you to New York.

You'll have one day to relax in Denver if you get there in time, which is what we want."

"Who made this plan?" I asked.

"Me," Selena responded. "See, I really like coming up with a plan and things like that. It's just always been my thing."

We said farewell and we left to the bus stop.

A few hours later, the sun was up but covered by a thick layer of clouds. The bus arrived and we headed in. The driver greeted us and led us to our seats.

"Look for monsters," Selena said. We watched as the people kept streaming in. There were a few weird looking people, a woman with a huge beehive haircut, a man who looked like a secret agent... I started drifting to sleep.

I kept watching sleepily. A girl with her mom, a short man with purple flames shooting from his mouth... wait, what? I bolted upright. Selena and Zach must have seen him too.

"A shadow ghoul," Selena gasped.

"Um... What do we do?"

"Just relax." Selena said, taking a deep breath. "Try to act normal. Ghouls have good smell, which isn't too useful. Their sight and hearing are bad."

"You smell like cinnamon..." I noted.

"That's my shampoo, okay? Now quiet!"

"Why can't the other people see him?"

"Abaddon masks all monsters from humans, and even sometimes from us," Zach said. "Just like Mrs. Key." The ghoul walked down the bus and sat right in front of us.

"Can you destroy him or something?" I whispered.

"They can only be destroyed in direct sunlight," Selena said. "It's overcast today. We can't."

That's great! I thought in my mind. *Now we're stuck in a bus, headed straight toward a shadow castle and there's a ghoul that we can't destroy in front of us.* We kept watch on the ghoul. Suddenly, a stream of sunlight broke out from the clouds.

"Now!" Selena whispered. The sunray lasered onto the ghoul.

I drew Malachite, and it elongated into a sword. I thrust the blade through the seat, and he screamed in pain and collapsed. Everyone looked up, and I quickly withdrew Malachite and hid it.

"What was that?" someone asked.

"Where did Mr. Scott go?" the person sitting next to him asked.

"Um, he went to use the restroom, I think," Selena said. Someone called the police, and they said they would investigate later when they stopped in Denver.

The man sitting in front of us turned his head and asked, "Did you kids see anything? You were sitting right behind him, so..."

"No..." I stammered. "I... uh... I was sleeping."

"Really?" the man said. "We'll have the police question you later..."

"But we really didn't..." I muttered.

"Don't worry," Selena said, but she didn't sound too sure. "Go sleep now." She leaned close to my ear and whispered, "you are also super bad liar, Will. But good try." I closed my eyes and immediately drifted into a dream.

...

I was back in Abaddon's castle. To be more accurate, I was outside of the castle.

I took my first good view of it. There was a huge main central tower, and I saw Abaddon, sitting in throne, at the top and only window. There were two big buildings connected to the central tower, one on the right and one on the left. There were large windows in the buildings overlooking a dark garden. The whole castle was situated on a mountain, and below it, many buildings and houses were scattered around in an unorderly fashion. A bleak black wall surrounded the whole fort, and there was a narrow bridge that led behind to the Empire State Building.

I wondered how nobody could see this huge hunky chunk of rock from below, but I guess Abaddon shaded human eyes from seeing it.

Suddenly, I started falling.

Below me, Selena held out her hands but she didn't catch me. Then, she morphed into Signus and laughed evilly. Right before I hit the ground, I woke up in a cold sweat.

...

Finally, after a long drive, (and many arguments between me and Selena), we arrived in Denver. While we were leaving the bus, the bus driver grabbed us by our arms.

"You're coming with me." His hands shriveled up into claws, and he waved them over our heads. A shimmering powder fell from his hands, and we immediately went to sleep.

...

"Uh..." I groaned. "Where... am I?" Selena and Zach lay sprawled on the stone floor. It was dark in the dungeon I was in. There were some iron bars on one side of the room, and the walls were gray, cracked, and crumbled. Growing on the walls was lots and lots of green moss. Selena and Zach were still alive, but they were still not completely conscious. The bus driver didn't disarm me for some reason, so I still had Malachite.

But Selena and Zach weren't the only ones making noise.

I heard some whimpering in a corner of the room.

"Um…hello?" I said uncertainly. I drew Malachite, and it cast a faint blue glow around the place. Then, I saw her. She had a thin face and wore faded blue clothes. She was crying and was wiping her face.

"Are you okay?" I asked.

"Yes...maybe…" she sniffled. "Could you… come closer… please?"

"Sure." I felt bad for this girl.

"So... how did you get here?" I asked.

"I was a descendant of Reality. I served him in Aquaia's court for many years-" She stopped and wiped a few tears.

"But he cursed me." Her voice changed from quiet and sad to loud and angry, "because I helped Abaddon. He bound me to this temple of Abaddon and turned me into a nymph!" She opened her hands, which revealed long, slender claws. She bared her teeth, which were fangs.

"So I destroy anyone who enters here!" She swiped Malachite from my hands, and it clattered to the ground before I could use it. She slammed me against the wall.

"Your gods are nothing compared to-"
Suddenly she screamed, and her body crumpled.
Standing behind her was Selena.

"Are you okay…" she asked.

"Yeah," I managed, but when I looked at my neck, I realized I was in no shape. It was bleeding and swollen from the nymph's tight grasp.

"Who was that thing?" I asked Selena.

"She was the head judge of Aquaia's court. But she helped Abaddon retrieve one of his favorite ghouls, so Reality cursed her. She was banished to this temple of Abaddon, and suffered in this dungeon for all eternity.

"The gods are really cruel sometimes."

"You better be careful with what you're saying there, dummy," Selena warned. 'The gods are not nice when you anger them."

"Where do monsters go after they're destroyed, anyway?"

"They don't actually die. Their spirit floats away to Signus, and he reforms them, and they appear right where they died in the same body. But right now, the monsters can't reform because you saw Signus steal Randy, and he couldn't possibly be back already."

"Is Zach conscious?" I asked.

"Ow…" I heard a moan.

"That's a yes," I grinned. "Let's get out of this place."

…

Our escape didn't go as planned.

Zach tried to use the moss to destroy the metal bars. It didn't even budge. So I took out Malachite and tried to cut it open. I made a tiny scratch, but at this rate, it would be past the deadline by the time we broke out. I heard voices coming from the hallway.

"-check on the prisoners." a voice said.

"Let's hope that they already got eaten by the nymph." The two monsters came into view. They both had on purple robes, and one was jangling some keys.

"Selena, can you use the wind here?" I asked.

"No, the air's too stagnant." She glared at me.

"Hey! I don't smell too-"

"They're awake!" the purple-robed man exclaimed. When they came closer, I realized that they were skeletons. He unlocked the cage.

"Oh, gosh darn it! We forgot to disarm them! Oh well. If you three could please put down your weapons, it would be awesome. If you do so, we'll give you ice cream after we sacrifice you to Abaddon," the other monster said. I drew Malachite and stuck the monster without the keys in the stomach.

"Ouch," he groaned, and collapsed in a pile of bones.

"He'll reform," the remaining skeleton said. "Okay, let's see…" He rummaged through his robe. "Oh! Here we go!" He brought out a purple book. I thought that he was going to read a nursery rhyme from it, but he opened it and started chanting words.

"No, no, no!" Zach screamed. But it was too late. The skeleton unleashed a blast of shadow. Luckily, it was misplaced, so he blasted off his foot and the half reformed skeleton.

"Oops!" the skeleton grinned. Selena sliced him in half with her wind blade, and we scampered out into the hallway. I took the spell tome and examined it.

"What is this thing in the first place?"

"Those spell tomes are the only way to actually destroy a skeleton, so keep it," Selena said to me.

"We can go left or right," Zach said. "Make a choice."

"Let's go left," Selena said.

"Why?"

"Because I can feel the fresher air that way."

"And when are you ever right in the first place?" I challenged.

"Just… I know it's the right way, okay? You two are allowed to go the other way, but I wouldn't recommend it. And also, you're making things difficult!"

"I love making things difficult, especially for you!" We cautiously snuck down the hallway.

Suddenly, I sensed something bad. I don't know how I did it, I just sort of felt like a trap was coming. I said, "Stop!"

"What?" Zach stopped but tripped and landed on a tripwire.

"Down!" I yelled, as heavy stone spears jabbed where our heads were.

"Definitely the right way," Zach grumbled, getting off the ground and brushing himself off.

"Hey! I know this leads to the outside, okay?" Selena argued.

"Sure, lead on, then." We turned the corner and I gasped. There was a shadow ghoul right in front of us. Looking back, we that another monster had blocked the way back.

"A necromancer!" Selena yelped. "This is so not good!"

"Are you really, really sure that this is the right way?" I asked. Then the necromancer attacked.

A beam of shadow energy blasted toward me. I moved, but it bounced off the wall and hit me.

"OW!" I screeched. My back exploded in pain, and I fell down. I drew Malachite and groaned, "Back off. We'll destroy you." The two monsters repelled from the sight of my dagger. I elongated it into a sword.

"Back off."

"The necromancer grinned. "I'm not scared. You're already dissolving." Sure enough, I looked at my back, and there was a good sized hole of darkness in it. I took out the spell tome. The monsters hesitated. I opened the book to a random page and began chanting the words.

Suddenly, a huge blast of lightning exploded from the book, and zapped the necromancer to ashes (which, by the way, does not really smell that great).

The ghoul roared and charged.

"What do we do?" I yelled. I felt my connection to the world growing fainter and fainter.

"There's no light!" Zach said. "But there might be a light spell in your book!"

"I'll keep him busy," Selena said, and became slashing and hacking the monster, although she wasn't doing any damage.

I saw a healing spell, and I kept my hand on that. There was a shadow spell, and finally, I found a light spell.

Selena cried out as the ghoul pinned her down, and Zach began wrestling with him.

I began chanting the words, and soon the book became dangerously bright. I aimed the beams at the ghoul, and Selena stuck her wind blade in the monster's skin. He cried out in pain and became limp at the feet of Selena.

"Gross," she cried, and kicked a slimy… never mind.

I went back to the healing spell, and began chanting words. Black splotches danced on my face. Finally, a warm red light glowed from the book, and I felt better.

"Let's continue," I said, but as soon as I stood up, I became dizzy and fell back down again.

"Zach," I groaned. "Can you… do the healing… spell?"

"Sure, I'll do it quick" but he was too slow, and I was captured in a vision.

…

I saw Fort Azari in the distance, but it looked different. There was a low, gray wall surrounding the property. Traps were set up around the area, and I spotted a new building that looked like an armory.

I floated in closer.

People rushing around, looking tense. The Corruption was getting closer and closer. A few demigods were outside, spreading powder on the corroded ground. "We've used all the powder!" someone cried.

"We still have time!" I heard Allen's voice yell. I guess he had taken command after Randy was… taken.

"Have you heard from Will and Selena?" Connor asked.

"No, but still, they won't give up that easily. We can do this!" Allen said. A cry resonated from the crowd, and for a moment, it sounded brave. Nina scowled and shook her head. Then, my vision faded away.

…

"You good?"

"Whoa!" I said. "I just had a vision, of Fort Azari. But it was like I was frozen in time!" I explained to them what had happened.

"Well, at least we know that they're preparing," Selena said. "That gives us some hope, I guess."

"Let's continue on," I said, and we headed down the corridor. There was a set of stairs leading upward.

"We're almost out!" I exclaimed. We walked out into fresh mountain air, and a net fell on top of us.

…

"You didn't think that you could escape that easily, did you?" a necromancer, seemingly the head, cackled He wore a long purple robe embroidered with sparkling jewels and gold.

"Where are we?"

"This is Mount Evans! We're still in Denver. That's good," Selena exclaimed.

"And how do you know that?" I asked.

"Just because I'm a girl and I'm pretty doesn't mean that I don't know anything!" she snapped.

"Okay, okay." To be honest, what she just said was making me really uncomfortable. I could feel myself turning red.

"But we're trapped now." There were four large columns supporting a domed roof. Under it, an altar that seemed to be for Abaddon sat. There were six other skeletal guards who held spears with shadowy tips.

"Explosion?" Selena whispered to me.

"I'll try." I closed my eyes and concentrated.

"No!" the necromancer growled, and blasted me with lightning. I flew back and Malachite clattered to the ground beside me. His eyes widened, and he used some kind of spell and disarmed us.

"Stupid," he muttered, "Forgot to disarm them."

"Now what?" I said. "We don't have any weapons, and we're stuck in a net. Have any plans?"

"Wait…" Selena closed her eyes, and a miniature tornado suddenly exploded out from her. It shredded the net and most of the monsters, and we ran out of the temple.

There was a nice little cabin sitting at the edge of a cliff. How odd.

"Let's go there," I said, pointing at the place. "They might have some information."

…

At least we could still catch the train to New York.

The old woman living in the house invited us in for some healthy disgusting herbal tea that tasted like the end of the world and asked us how we got here.

"We got lost when we were hiking," I explained.

"Also," Zach asked, "what's the date and the time?"

"Oh!" the lady exclaimed. "It's the tenth of June right now, and it's seven in the morning." I breathed a sigh of relief. It was still five days from the deadline. Because it was the morning, we could still catch the train.

"Well," Selena said. "We gotta go…"

"Wait, just a moment." She held up her hands. "I want to show you my dogs! I've been training them for years now!"

She brought us outside and around the back. There was a cliff on one side, and I saw a pathway leading down.

"Um… ma'am," Selena continued. "We really, really need to hurry. Can we see them later?"

"Just a moment…" she snapped her fingers and the ground exploded in ice. Her hands were blue and cold and she held a staff of frost in her hands. I looked up at her face. It wasn't old at all. All the creases were gone and now replaced with evil, frosty glare.

"Here are my dogs!" she announced, and she waved her staff. Three icy dogs formed from the snow beneath her feet and started barking and snarling at us. "I am Cryos, the goddess of ice."

"Are they friendly?" I asked. "Because… whoa!" One of the dogs lunged at me and knocked me into the snow. He was gnawing on my shirt and scratching my face, which did not feel that good.

"Get off my friend!" Zach yelled. He kicked him away (and almost kicked me). I drew Malachite, and slashed at the first dog. It exploded into ice, but it froze my hand. Cryos advanced and launched a full force blizzard at me. I got hit and was knocked thirty feet back in the air. Cryos pointed a crooked finger at Zach, and he froze into an ice cube. The other two dogs launched at us. Selena drew her weapon, a wind blade, and blew the dog away.

"Why are you attacking us, anyway?" I demanded. "We just requested some information!"

"Because you attacked my harmless dogs! So I needed to protect them, right?"

"Yeah! But that's because one of your dogs jumped on top of me and started biting me!"

"He was trying to show that he likes you!" she explained.

"Will! Cryos attacks anyone who comes close to her! And we can't do anything about it!"

"You try to do something then," I said back.

"Okay." She took a deep breath and closed her eyes.

"You stop now!" Cryos commanded. "She summoned an ice dagger and prepared to throw it at Zach.

"This ends no-" A huge blast of air blew Cryos off her feet. I turned and saw Selena, floating on a storm cloud. She blasted Cryos off the cliff.

"Nooooo!" she screamed. Her two dogs stopped trying to eat us and bowed to Selena.

"I think that they're mine now," Selena said. One of the dogs nodded in response.

"Good. Could you unfreeze Will and Zach?" The dogs bounded up to me and licked my hands. They unfroze and I shook them. The dogs then ran up to Zach and unfroze him.

"I think I can fly us down the mountain," Selena said. "Hop on."

...

It took us four hours to get down the mountain. Selena nearly collapsed because of the effort. Luckily, the train station was right in front of us.

"Well," I said. "Our ride is here." We hopped on the train just as it pulled away from the station.

"And we have some quality time ahead of us," Zach said.

Chapter 3

We slept in our seats for a while, but then we were hungry. We headed down for dinner in the dining room, and the food was great. But my appetite changed when I saw the bus driver that drove us to Denver.

"The bus driver's here," I whispered to Selena.

"Oh gosh!" she said, and slumped back in her chair. "How… Oh no," People kept leaving until there was only us and the ghoul left.

"Hello," the ghoul said. I drew Malachite.

"Oh, but as you know, ghouls can only be destroyed in broad daylight. I don't think that can happen right now."

"Selena," I whispered. "Do you have any amazing plan right now?"

"Maybe… Just keep him occupied for a bit. Zach, I'll need you."

"And also I can cast spells. You don't want to get near me." To show his amazing skills, he burst a hanging chandelier into a million shards. They rained down onto the carpet and stuck there like spikes.

"So," I said casually, trying to distract him. "Can you blow flames, too?"

"Sure I can! Watch!" he torched a table.

"Wow! You're amazing. So, what are you here for?"

"Oh," he said. "I have to keep watch on you three. Sadly, there are no other monsters on the train here."

"That's a bummer."

"Yeah! Definitely."

"Got it!" Selena exclaimed.

"Got what?" the ghoul asked suspiciously. But then, the ghoul realized. Selena started to brighten. Then, she filled the room with a blinding light. The ghoul screamed in agony.

"Stop! My eyes!" I quickly sprinted forward and swung Malachite. I wasn't even close to him, but a blue sword projectile flew out and sliced him.

"I'm...losing... control!" Selena screamed.

"I can't stop" But she exploded in light.

...

We were strewn across a field. The train had stopped. Police cars and ambulances surrounded the wreckage. I heard the train conductor say, "We'll get everyone a coupon for three hundred dollars for what happened. Come get them here!" We ran up quickly, grabbed three, and left. I saw the St. Louis arch up ahead.

"At least we crashed in a convenient spot," I said.

"Okay," Zach said. "Let's go."

. . .

"Where should we go?" I wondered, once we entered into St. Louis.

"The Arch!" Selena and Zach said simultaneously.

"Really? That's all? We could go to some restaurant and... you know..."

"We just had dinner, man," Zach said, brushing away a lock of his long black hair.

We walked past shops and buildings. I saw in a television store a T.V. that was showing where the train that had crashed.

"Massive damage done to the train, some sort of acid has destroyed most of the train's engine. So, Steve, we have from the train wreck here except for three adolescent children and an older gentleman. They were also reported to be the only ones left in the dining room. We still aren't sure what happened. Are the children the culprit or the man? Or is it someone completely different? We'll find out later after a commercial break." Selena pulled me away before I could tell the reporters how wrong they were. We saw the Arch up ahead and entered into it.

"Something's not right," Zach said. He looked around nervously.

"What?"

"I don't know..."

"We're just confused after the train wreck, Zach. Nothing's wrong. Don't worry." Zach still looked around nervously.

We headed into the cramped elevator that would take us to the top. There was another girl who looked about a year older than us in the elevator. She had flowing blond hair and sea blue eyes that, just like Randy, seemed to have a fiery glint in them. She smiled at me, and I blushed. Somehow, she looked familiar, like some celebrity or something. Selena muttered, "I don't trust her."

"I like your dogs," she said.

"How can she see them?" Selena whispered.

"Where are your parents?" I asked nervously.

"Oh..." Her face darkened, and, was it my imagination, or did her hands spark?

"My name's Sarah," she said.

"Okay. My name's Will. This is Selena, and this is Zach." Suddenly, the elevator dinged, and we walked out to the top. Only a short man and a woman were on the observation deck. They turned smiled at us. In the man's mouth, flames flickered.

"What's that?" I whispered to Selena. "Are we in trouble again?"

"A plague ghoul, don't get close to him. He radiates sickness. We really should get going now."

"Okay." The ghoul grinned. The woman next to him shriveled up and turned into a nymph.

"Hello." They said in unison.

"Oh no," Zach said. "They're mechanical, which means that we can't destroy them."

"That might be a problem," I said, "Just a small problem."

"Come Sarah," the nymph said to Sarah, who flinched.

"Stop!" I called. Sarah opened her hands. The nymph put her claws to Sarah's neck and held her there.

"One step closer," she snarled. "And she'll be dead!" Suddenly, Sarah's hands exploded with fire, and the nymph was burnt to a crisp. Sarah crumpled because of the effort.

"I'll get you for this!" the plague ghoul screamed, and blasted Sarah with toxic fumes.

"No!" I yelled. The poison had burnt through the Arch, and there was no way Sarah could have survived. Meanwhile, the nymph was still alive, but her outside skin was charred off and uncovered the metallic uncovering.

"I'm not dead yet!" the nymph cackled. She charged along with the ghoul. Selena whacked the nymph with her wind blade and willed the air to push her of the hole in the Arch.

I looked at Sarah and saw that she wasn't turned into toast. She barely looked hurt at all. Her shirt was smoking, but it seemed like no harm had come to her.

Meanwhile, Zach was fending off the ghoul by blasting him with a green light and growing vines around him. I drew Malachite and charged. I shot blue sword projectiles at him, but it just bounced off her tough hide. Selena tried to hack at him with her wind blade.

We were tiring, but the ghoul just wouldn't stop. He blew acid at us, but Selena launched it away back at him. The acid burned away his outer covering of skin, and underneath it was a mechanical frame.

"Not immune to his own powers." I muttered. The ghoul screamed and tried to blast poison, put his skull was burning away. I whacked him with Malachite, and he fell off the observation deck. I ran up to Sarah.

"Are...you okay?" Police sirens started wailing, and Sarah stirred.

"What...happened?" she croaked.

"You destroyed a nymph," I said. The elevator dinged, and two cops rushed out.

"Stop!" one of them yelled. "What did you do to this girl?"

"Let's go, Selena!" I called. I grabbed Sarah, and jumped off the edge of the Arch.

...

Water has never been good to me.

I saw Selena, riding the winds with Zach, floating along as happy as can be.

Me? What was I doing?

I was screaming for my life as I fell toward the water. Because I was an elemental, I knew that I could control water, but with a fire user right next to me, I'm not so sure.

I tried to concentrate on the water, and used all my might. The water seemed to do nothing, but it really softened my fall. We landed with a huge splash which probably wouldn't have gotten us a high score in Olympic diving, and sank to the bottom.

And now I wish the water was a bit cleaner.

There was gross garbage, old shoes, tin cans, and many other things I don't want to mention in there. I swam out as quickly as possible and took a deep breath, surveying the destruction we made (I'm blaming Selena and Zach, okay). The Arch was still on fire, and soon it would become two separate sticks of metal poking out of the ground. Ambulances and police cars completely surrounded destroyed piece of architecture (although I personally liked the flaming Arch better). I heard a news reporter standing near the wreckage.

"Think that they are the same people who were not found in the train crash near here. They seemed to have taken another girl with them. We don't know if the adolescent children caused the flames, or if they're being held hostage for something. News reports say that the boy with black hair is called Will Hanson. We don't know anything about the other three children, but if you see them, please dial 911 right away."

"Stupid," I muttered, and walked away.

I set Sarah down and waited for her to become fully conscious.

"What-what happened?" she groaned. I explained to her that she had blasted the nymph with fire, and then had collapsed.

"So… where are your parents?"

"I… I really don't want to talk about it right now. Please. Just… let me take a breath."

"We have to go search for Selena and Zach now," I said. We stood up and started walking.

"By the way, I just thought I'd mention it. Thanks for saving me." She smiled gratefully. "I never knew if there were people like me, but now I know." I nodded back. "You're definitely welcome to stay with us, if you like."

"I 'd appreciate that." She brushed a lock of her golden hait behind her ear, and we set off in search of Selena and Zach.

Chapter 4

Selena and Zach found us. They were walking the streets, and they saw us while we were stopping at a coffee place.

"Are you okay?" Selena asked.

"We jumped off and destroyed a National monument, but we're fine."

"When Selena flew us across the river, she passed afterwards, but we're okay now," Zach said.

"So, Sarah. How did you get here?"

"Well, my dad said that I could wander off wherever I want to today, so I went to the Arch. This is sort of creepy though, because I had a dream that I would meet you." *What kind of dad is that?* I thought in my head. Maybe that's the reason she didn't want to talk about it now.

"What else?" Selena asked.

"A voice said that I would go with you all to Richmond to seek advice from someone. We were supposed to ask him where some key is hidden."

"Did the key look as dark as night?" Zach asked.

"Yes."

"It's still about four days from the deadline," I said. "We can do it."

"But isn't your dad going to notice?" Selena asked.

"No, He won't."

"But how do we get there?" Selena wondered.

"I'll take care of that, I guess." Sarah sighed and walked off.

...

A few minutes later, we were cruising in a comfortable luxury car. How did Sarah do it? She just walked up to a taxi driver, told him her name, and bam!

"Who's your dad?" I said once we were in the car. Sarah's face darkened.

"Oh, sorry..." I muttered.

"Sorry... I should tell you. My full name's Sarah Miller. My dad is John Miller. He's a famous spokesperson, you know. That show..."

"John Miller?" Selena and Zach yelped at once.

"No way!" Zach seemed really excited. "Can I have his signature? That would be so cool-"

"Wait a minute, guys. Who is he?" I asked, feeling pretty stupid.

"You don't... you're hopeless," Selena decided. "You've never ever heard of him before? Ever?"

"Um..."

"Yeah," Sarah grumbled. "Big deal, I don't really don't care. He barely notices me anyway."

"You don't-"

"Well," I interrupted. "Better rest up, we have a long day ahead." I closed my eyes and put my head against the cushioned seat.

"Good night." Selena said, and patted my shoulder. "You'll get more intelligent someday." I fell into a deep sleep that was interrupted by my worst dream yet.

...

I saw Randy, all chained up in Abaddon's palace. His face was bloody and his clothes were torn up. He seemed to be half made of shadow, like he wasn't totally living in this world.

I looked at the room he was in. It must have been the room I saw Abaddon in my latest dream. There were intricate pillars that reached up so far that I couldn't see the end of them. There were two windows, actually, and they were parallel from each other. No one else was in the room at the moment. The Key of Nightmares wasn't in the room either.

I wanted to cry out to him, but my voice wouldn't work.

"So dark..." He moaned. "Light... Light! Abaddon... cursed - too dark!" He went on crying out.

The darkness must be driving him nuts! I thought. *We have to hurry.*

Then, my dream changed.

...

I saw a smoky palace in the distance. The stones used to make it were smoking red. Banners were hung up everywhere. It must have been the symbol of Yharon. The banner was pale yellow, with an orange dot in the middle. There was a spiky crown on top of the dot, and below it was a brown V shape.

I floated in closer.

Then I saw the palace. There was a huge dome in the center of four long rectangular buildings. Around it, there was a huge garden area with fiery flowers, flaming trees, and other crazy plants.

I floated in toward the dome, and I saw that there was an open area near the top of the dome. Abaddon and Yharon were sitting at the top. Yharon was wearing a red suit this time. His eyes were molten flames, and this time his hair was a flowing red-hot inferno.

"We have lured them right into the trap," Yharon said. "Soon, the girl and the protector will be dead, and the elemental will fight for our cause."

"What if he refuses?" Abaddon mentioned.

"We have the leader. He can't fight against that."

"Okay. I'm staying here for a bit longer. Quite possibly the next couple days, I think that Signus has got it under control." A flood of relief washed over me. Five days. We could do this. My dream faded away.

...

I woke up. We were still cruising along the highway in the middle of the forest and it was raining.

"Where are we?" I yawned. Selena, Sarah, and Zach all were awake.

"We entered Virginia a while ago," Selena said. "It's about nine in the morning currently, and we're almost at Richmond."

"Perfect weather," I muttered, and then remembered my dream. "I had a dream."

"What?" Sarah laughed. "Are you gonna recite Martin Luther King's speech?"

"No," I snorted.

"A dream," Zach said. "Dreams are really important."

"Are they actually true, though?" Sarah asked.

"Yes," Selena answered. "Now talk about it."

"Well, first, I saw Randy, chained up in Abaddon's palace. It looked like he was going crazy."

"Oh no!" Selena said. "Well then, the deadline might be a bit closer than we thought. But he'll be able to hold on for longer. I trust him."

"Who's Randy?" Sarah wondered. Selena told her all about Fort Azari.

"Wow. So there's actually a place where demigods can live in peace?" She gazed off into the distance as if she was trying to imagine how it would be like.

"And then my dream shifted."

"Okay," Zach said.

"I saw Yharon's palace. Abaddon was with him. And now I have good news and bad news. Which do you want to hear first?"

"Good news!" they all said simultaneously.

"Well, Abaddon will be staying at Yharon's palace for five more days, so we'll be safe. Signus also is a bit delayed, so we should be free to go."

"Cool," Selena said.

"And the bad news?" Zach asked.

"Yharon said that we've been led right into a trap."

"But what kind of trap?" Sarah said.

"What about you?" Selena suddenly spoke, turning to Sarah. "How do we know that you're not leading us into a trap?"

"Well," Sarah said. "You have to trust me. Really, I'm not."

"But how can we trust you? You-"

"Stop!" I yelled. "We just have to trust each other. We can't go around just thinking that everyone's an enemy!"

"Okay," Selena said, calmed down. She took a deep breath. "Okay. Sorry." The car pulled to a stop.

"We're here!" the taxi driver called, pulling down the privacy glass window that separated us.

"It's just forest all around us," Sarah said in wonder. "How are we going to find this guy?"

"I think I know," Zach said.

"Let's go find someone under the rain. Yay," Selena muttered.

...

The crazy chickens helped us find him.

Zach led us to the town, and I saw a flash of lightning fly up into the sky.

"What was that?" I said. Then I heard something that sounded like a lot of chickens. We turned a corner.

Then, we saw it.

There were about twenty flying birds attacking something. The birds looked like eagles, with yellow and blue feathers. They buzzed with electricity and every so often fired a blast of lightning at the something. There were a few picnic tables scattered around the area.

"Thunderbirds!" Selena gasped. "It's been a really long time since I've since one of the."

"Lead the birds away," I whispered to Zach.

"Okay." Zach whistled and called all the birds to him.

"Over here!" The birds revealed an old, fat man wearing a flowery robe and pajamas. His hair was messed up and charred, probably what the birds did to him. He was having his breakfast of potatoes and bacon and he grinned at us.

"Hello, friends!"

"What's with this guy?" I murmured to Selena.

"What's with this guy?" the man boomed. "No hello? Well, that's rude! Well, I'm sorry for you to know, but I have exceptional hearing, but not an exceptional amount of sight. If only I could get those scorpions, then I'd be good."

"What?"

"Well, my name's Aggergard. I was Abaddon's helper in the past days. But now Signus took my place... I only was cursed by him because I was too lazy. Always lay on the couch too much. But when we release Oblivion, he'll send his wrath upon that annoying Signus." He sniffed the air, wrinkled his nose, and went back to eating his breakfast. Just then, Zach returned. "I led them away."

"We've come here to ask for information," Selena said promptly.

"Okay! Sure! What do you want?"

"We want to know where the Key of Nightmares is," Zach said.

"The key! Oh… Wait, let me sense it!" He closed his eyes in concentration. After a few seconds, he said: "Oh! I see it! It's in- Wait. You need to give me something in exchange."

"What is it?"

"In Florida, there is Scorpio. He holds some scorpions that I can use to finally kill these annoying thunderbirds!"

"Well, how do we get there and back?" I snapped.

"You can take an airplane. Or I can teleport you. I can give you a rope to lasso the scorpion. Once you get one, you'll teleport back immediately, but only two people, only two. Who do you choose?"

"We need Will," Zach said. "Who else?"

"Not me!" Sarah backed up. "I can't stand seeing bugs. They gross me out and scare me."

"I can go, if you're fine with that," Selena said.

"Sure then," Sarah said. "Stay safe. Don't get eaten by a bunch of humongous scorpion bugs." She shuddered. "I hate scorpions, or any other type of bug."

"Bye!" Zach called.

"Okay then," Aggergard said. "Let's go! Hold your hands please."

"What?" we said in unison. My face was bright red.

"Come on!" Sarah said.

"Okay, then," Selena grumbled. She looked at me. "Ready?"

"Definitely not!" We linked hands. "Let's go." Aggergard closed his eyes in concentration and threw his hands in the air.

The world turned upside down, and we were in Florida, with two beady eyes staring right at us.

...

"Well, I guess we found Scorpio already," I muttered. We were immediately bound with ropes and disarmed, and we were now being carried along a street by bloodthirsty mutated scorpions.

They dumped us down in a building that was labelled Scorpion Inc... There was a front lobby with regular milling around, checking their phones. I guess Abaddon was doing his job, maybe a bit too well, because the people didn't notice a thing. We were led down a corridor to a room labelled Packing and Shipping.

The room we entered was huge. And I mean huge. It extended about one hundred feet into the air. It was probably twice the length across, and I couldn't even see to the end. There were random boxes scattered all over the floor, some holding water bottles and some holding spears. Large racks with materials in them stood at the left of where we entered. There were platforms fifty feet in the air, and I saw prison cells up there. Good, I thought.

Selena is good with the air. I saw a huge table, bigger than a bear in the right side of the room. Behind it, a scorpion way bigger than all the rest sat reclining in a comfy chair.

I thought that the scorpions were big enough. Someone probably wanted a bigger one.

This one was the size of an elephant. I didn't think that it could see us from all the way back there, but its beady eyes fixed on us. Its two pincers clicked in delight.

"Oh, fun," Selena groaned. One of the scorpions whacked her on the head with one of its claws. She cried out in pain and looked at me helplessly. I thought that scorpions could only talk in scorpion language, but it spoke in a raspy voice: "You don't want to anger us, do you? Careful with what you say." Other scorpion laughed and said: "C'mon, Joe. Be nice to them."

"Come over!" the big scorpion, who was probably Scorpio, said.

"We got them!" Joe cackled.

"Well, well, well," Scorpio said. "Well, we'll take you to our cages. I hope you enjoy your stay."

. . .

We were taken to the second level in the room, shut in a cage, and were tied together so that our backs were against each other and we couldn't turn around.

"They put our stuff in the room next to here," Selena said.

"Really, how did you do?"

"We have eyes, dummy. And I have pretty good eyesight. Could you, like, blast us out of here and back to Virginia, please?"

"We could try to do it, but I don't think I have enough energy to do it again."

"Try to do a little one, maybe."

"Okay." I concentrated and summoned two elemental daggers.

"Nice," she said. I gave a dagger to her.

"Let's not get free yet," I said. "We need a plan first. Like what you do all the time. You just come up with plans."

"Look at that!" Selena joked. "Someone's actually using his brain today. If he had a brain in the first place" I tried to punch her, which was pretty difficult to do while tied up.

"Ouch," she laughed.

"Okay," I said. "So, we need to get the rope and tie a scorpion. Then we leave. Easy."

"So you don't have a plan after all."

"Yeah."

"Okay, then. Let's go." We slowly cut the ropes.

"Okay," Selena said. "Slowly move toward the room." We edged closer and closer. Finally, I said, "Go!" We jumped up and slashed through the metal bars like cheese (yum!).

"What-" a scorpion screamed as we pushed it off the platform. It smashed into two other scorpions, and they tumbled into a support beam holding up the platform we were on.

"Uh oh," I said. The walkway groaned and threatened to collapse. We grabbed our weapons and the rope and sprinted out of the room. The alarm started to blare, and the scorpions on the walkway turned. We were trapped.

They advanced slowly and raised their tails.

"Don't get hit by the stinger," Selena warned.

"Okay." One scorpion fired, and it glanced off Malachite and ricocheted into the ground, which didn't help make the walkway more stable

"I didn't know that they could shoot stingers," I complained.

"Well they do, it's not my fault!"

"Stop where you are!" one scorpion said. "We have our stingers pointed at you."

"No thanks," I yelled, and blasted them all with elemental energy. It barely fazed them, but one of them fell and landed on a box labeled *Bombs*.

"Oh no," I muttered, and started running along with Selena to another platform. There was a huge explosion, and we got thrown forward. The platform started to collapse, and we started falling. I was caught by Selena on a cloud that she made, and we floated upward.

Stingers shot from all directions, and I launched some of Malachite's beams down at the scorpions.

But Selena was tiring. Her movements started to slow down, and soon we had to drop on what was left of the walkway. Scorpio came to where we were and grinned (if scorpions can grin) up at us.

"Why don't you come down? We won't hurt you. It will be a quick and painless death."

"No thanks," I muttered, and fired another blue projectile down at him, and it made a dent in his head. Scorpio roared.

"Are you holding up fine?" I asked Selena.

"Maybe," she groaned her face was turning red. "I don't know if I can hold it up any longer."

"I will shoot the platform down!" Scorpio threatened.

"But how do we get down?" I asked, trying to burn through time.

"Well, hmm… you ask good questions. We could purchase a crane… but that's not worth it. Nah. We'll do it the easy way." He shot a huge dark stinger at the platform, and it exploded. The bridge we were on started bending. And with a sickening crack, the platform fell down with us, fifty feet in the air, toward a group of deadly scorpions.

…

How did we survive the fall? Well, Selena is absolutely amazing. She controlled the air just enough for us not to break every bone in our bodies.

"Who should we eat first?" Scorpio boomed. The scorpions started screaming suggestions.

"The girl, deep fried!"

"The boy, baked!"

"I want them both medium rare!"

"Silence!" Scorpio roared. "Set the fire!" Two scorpions rushed forward and made a huge, blazing campfire.

"Can we roast them alive?" one scorpion pleaded.

"No!" Scorpio bellowed. Just then, I remembered that they had forgotten to disarm us. It wasn't a big advantage, but it was a small advantage.

"We'll have Joe, who found these two, decide what to do with them!" Scorpio continued. Joe stepped forward and readied his stinger. I closed my eyes. He shot.

A clump of vines dragged the stinger to the side. Suddenly, fire leaped through the air and burned him.

"Aaaaagggghhh!" he screamed in agony. Zach and Sarah appeared through the door.

"Grab a scorpion!" Sarah yelled. I wrestled a huge black one down, and I tied the rope around it.

My vision started to go blurry, and I saw that we weren't teleporting.

"Everyone needs to hold on to this rope!" I screamed, as the scorpion whipped his head around. Selena came and held on, but Zach and Sarah were getting cornered by Scorpio. Selena used her last bit of energy to launch them over the scorpion's head, and she slumped down.

"Come on!" I said. I grabbed Selena from slipping off the rope.

"We're here!" Sarah yelled. "Oh, gosh. I hate seeing bugs."

"Okay!" The scorpions turned and charged us and almost got us. But, the world turned upside down, and we disappeared from their deadly grasp with one of their scorpions.

…

"We're back!" Sarah hollered.

"You survived!" Aggergard bellowed heartily under a cloud of thunderbirds. "Well, I wish you were eaten, but sure. Thanks for the scorpion!"

"Give us the information now!" Zach demanded.

"Okay, okay, I'll write it down." He gave the note to me, and it said: hidden behind throne in throne room.

"All that work for this," Sarah muttered.

"Let's relax for a bit, shall we?" I said. We headed over to a restaurant and set Selena down.

"So, how did you get to Florida?" I asked.

"Oh!" Sarah said. "We begged Aggergard to let us go too, and soon he got so annoyed that he just let in."

"It's only one o'clock right now. Problem with Abaddon's fortress is that you can only access it at night." Zach said.

"Oh," Sarah said. "So, should we try for tomorrow night? If so, we would still have two days left. There's no rush. We can do this."

"Do you think that you could get another taxi?" I asked.

"Okay then. Just wait here." And she jogged off.

…

This time, the car was even fancier. We were in a Tesla Model X. Selena and I sat in the back next to each other, while Sarah and Zach sat the middle row.

"Guys, can we go to Philadelphia first before we go to New York City?

"Let's get some more sleep, because we'll have a long day… or night ahead," Zach said.

"Yeah," Selena said. "It'll be about five or six o'clock when we get there. Maybe Sarah can find us a hotel to sleep in."

"Yeah. We'll see." She didn't seem as cheerful as usual, and for some reason, it looked like she was about to cry.

"Have a good sleep then," I said.

I closed my eyes, and I felt Selena's head on my shoulder. I fell into a perfect sleep that was ruined by another nightmare.

Chapter 5

I saw Abaddon's fortress in the distance.

A voice from the sky said: "The trap had been set." There it was again. The trap, whatever it was.

I came in closer, and I saw Randy. His eyes were closed, and he was slumped over. No way, I thought. But he groaned, and I knew there still was hope. His body was covered in shadow, so I knew we had to hurry. If we waited too long, he would dissolve.

I thought I saw something moving in the shadows of the room, but when I looked up, there was no one. It was probably my imagination.

Randy cried out in pain, and my dream changed.

...

I was back at Yharon's palace and heard a roaring sound from inside the building. Yharon was sitting on the rooftop patio with Abaddon, drinking tea.

"She's waking," Abaddon said.

"Yes. Finally, after being harmed for so long, we will finally unleash her onto Fort Azari."

"How did she get hurt the first time?" Abaddon asked. Yharon's eyes flared and Abaddon flinched. I thought that Abaddon was scary enough, but Yharon was much more powerful. I wondered how I could ever face off Oblivion.

"There was a stupid girl, tried to save her mom. My…" He trailed off.

"Okay, then," Abaddon said quickly, trying to change the topic. "Fort Azari won't stand a chance. Let's go back in." I thought that my dream was over, but I followed them down into the palace.

The inside was incredible.

They were in a long hallway, and the floor had red carpet on it. There were crystal chandeliers hanging from the ceiling, which was way up. Many doors lined the hallway, and there were also big columns that indicated a turn in the hallway. So many doors, I thought. And only one room has Vesuvius in it.

Yharon led Abaddon to a turn in the hallway, and what I saw blew my mind.

It was obviously the throne room.

The throne itself had a red cushion and was studded with glimmering rubies. I saw an intricate design on the backrest. It looked like a stick, with some kind of orb and runes floating at the end of it. Vesuvius.

Even in my dream, I felt it radiating power. Now I knew why no one could find it. It was almost impossible to get.

The ceiling was so high up that I couldn't even see it. But, more crystal chandeliers were visible hanging down. There were windows facing outwards into the garden. I figured that we were still in the main tower, and this room took up one-fourth of the floor.

I saw a jungle outside of the fiery keep and the walls. A river ran through the trees. So peaceful, I thought. Compared to what we were in now.

There were flaming torches lining the curved walls. The floor was the most interesting. It was a mosaic that kept on changing. First, it showed an aerial view of Yharon's castle. Then, it changed, and a picture of a dragon appeared. I first thought that it was just an image, but I soon saw that the stones were shifting under Yharon and Abaddon's feet.

Suddenly, Yharon looked up right at me.

At first, I thought that he was just looking at something behind me, but his piercing stare was obviously looking at me.

"Abaddon," Yharon growled. "Your senses have been dulled. You do command over dreams, do you?"

"Yes, my lord."

"Well, you should know better than to let an eavesdropper in!" He raised his hands and sent a beam of fire right at me.

...

I jolted awake.

"What… what was that?" Selena yawned.

"Oh, sorry." I forgot that Selena had slept against me.

"Did you have a good sleep?" I said. "Because I really didn't. I told Selena about my dream.

"And we're stuck in traffic? Really? Oh well."

"Yeah… we are… what?" a sleepy voice said from in front of us.

"Zach, you're awake too?" Selena laughed.

"Yeah."

"I'm awake also," Sarah announced.

"I had another dream," I announced. I told them about Randy and Yharon, but I left out the part about the dragon.

"I think that'll be the last dream we'll get in a while," I muttered.

"So, Sarah, where do you want to visit?" Zach asked, changed the topic.

"I - well - I want to visit the Liberty Bell." From her voice and my dream, I knew that Sarah was keeping something behind my back.

"Sure!" Zach yawned. "We have time," Selena whispered to me. "Didn't John Miller's wife die somehow in Philadelphia?"

"Why would I know? As I said, I had no idea who John Miller was until now. So why would I know who his wife was?"

"I don't know," She shrugged and looked out the window.

...

We arrived at the Liberty Bell at six o'clock. But getting there was another matter. We ran into loads of shadow enemies while getting to the Bell.

Luckily, Selena's two dogs, which were now named Nimbus and Cryus, sniffed them out.

First, we saw a party of shadow ghouls, drinking at a pub. They turned to our attention and started chasing us. They might have gotten us if they weren't that drunk, but that's what they get. I drew my spell tome and summoned light again, while Selena sliced them to pieces.

Another time, we got surrounded by nymphs under a necromancer. The necromancer summoned a bunch of fake monsters to confuse us.

But, Sarah blasted the necromancer with fire, and the illusions stopped. We then ran past them and moved on.

"Why are there so many monsters around here?" I complained.

"One, because it's night, and two, because it's so close to Abaddon's fortress, so many monsters are safer here." Selena answered.

"You know a lot for an airhead," I said.

"Hey!" We all laughed, except for Sarah, which was kind of weird, because she liked to laugh.

"Just kidding," I just wanted to know the real reason Sarah wanted to go here, so I burst out.

"Sarah. Why do you want to see the Liberty Bell?" She glanced away, so I said: "You don't have to tell us. It just"

"Okay. I'll tell you."

"There's the Liberty Bell, just ahead," I announced. Suddenly, someone just materialized in front of me, and I walked right through her. She had blue eyes and blond hair just like Sarah. She was Sarah's mom.

"Mom!" Sarah yelled.

"I'm not actually here, dear."

"No, mom!" Tears welled up in her eyes. Sarah's mom raised her hands as if to cast a spell. And then, we were caught in a trance.

...

We were somewhere else in Philadelphia. We weren't ghosts, but no one could see us.

I saw Sarah, a bit younger, running ahead. Her mom was standing next to her, holding her hand. We moved forward, and we saw the Liberty Bell in the distance.

"-have to go, dear," her mom was saying.

"No!" Sarah argued.

"He'll take you otherwise."

"He'll take me, even if you turn yourself over to him! Don't!" Sarah protested.

"I have to." There was a roar from the area of the Liberty Bell.

"His dragon is waiting. Be safe, dear."

"NO!" Sarah's mom looked down in shame.

"I'm very sorry. But I have to go." A building crumbled in the distance.

"The dragon will destroy the whole city if I don't go. I love you." Sarah's mom ran off. A tear streaked down Sarah's cheek. But her face turned angry. She started to turn red.

"How dare him… My own mother!" she screamed. Suddenly, she burst into red-hot flames, and her back sprouted burning wings. She launched into the air and saw the dragon lift off.

The dragon was one hundred percent the one I heard in my dream.

If you haven't seen this dragon, you haven't seen scary. This dragon was huge. She easily was bigger than a house. She had red hot scales, and had balls of fire as eyes. Her tail looked like a blazing whip, studded with deadly spikes. Her wings were enormous, and they looked like Sarah's except that they were forty times larger. For some reason, there were vines hanging from the dragon's wings. Sarah's mom sat atop a red saddle on the dragon.

The dragon blew fire in the air and smashed down more buildings.

"I have… to… stop it!" Sarah gritted her teeth and launched herself toward the dragon. She summoned a flaming dagger and threw it into her eyes. It stuck there, and she got the dragon's attention. The dragon roared and blew flames at Sarah. Its tail whipped around and tried to smack her, but she dodged it.

"I gotta lead it away…" she muttered. She summoned more daggers and fired them at the dragon, but it seemed to just annoy her.

"SAVE YOURSELF!" Sarah's mom screamed. Sarah flew forward and led the dragon away from the big city. Sarah closed her eyes and took a deep breath. Suddenly, a storm of deadly fire spikes rained from the sky and impaled themselves into the dragon. It roared and spun in a circle, lashing its tail out.

"Hang on!" she yelled to her mom.

"NO! Honey, leave now! This is for your own good. You'll get yourself killed!"

"I won't leave you to your father!" Sarah yelled back. My heart skipped a beat. Yharon. Yharon was Sarah's… grandfather? Now that was weird. Selena, next to me grabbed my hand. In normal circumstances, I would be embarrassed, but this was very frightening.

Sarah was doing good, but she was tiring. Sweat dripped off her face. She paused for a moment, and that was her fatal mistake.

The dragon whipped her tail around and smacked Sarah in the back. She cried out in pain and tried to keep her wings intact on her back. They were rapidly dissolving, and she put all her strength to leap onto the dragon. Her wings dissipated just as she reached the dragon.

The dragon flew forward in a burst, and Sarah only caught onto one of her vines hanging from her wings.

"Ahhh!" she screamed, but I guess the vines were the dragon's life source, because she roared in pain and veered toward the ground.

They landed on a grassy plain in the middle of nowhere.

The dragon smashed against the earth and tried to blast Sarah with fireballs. One caught her in the face, but that just energized her.

"NO SARAH!" her mom yelled. Her voice was so loud that Sarah even paused for a second.

"Help me, mom!" Sarah cried. "Please!" The dragon was still flailing around in the dirt, and Sarah was using all her might to stay attached to the dragon's vines.

"No! Sarah, run!"

"MOM! HELP ME!" Sarah screamed. She exploded in light and ripped off the vine. The dragon bellowed and tried to hit Sarah, but she was growing dangerously bright. Tendrils of flame leaped out of her and shocked the dragon. Her whole body was on fire.

"Okay." her mom said. She took a deep breath and summoned flame wings. She shot fireballs at the dragon, but it wasn't doing much.

"Hit the dragon's vines!" Sarah called, herself bolting for the plants. She shot a searing white flame at a vine, and burned it straight off. The dragon whipped around and blew flames right into her face. The dragon flew off, but Sarah and her mom pursued her.

Sarah now could float off the ground on a hover board of fire. She concentrated again and summoned a firestorm from the sky. The red-hot flames pelted the dragon's skin and lodged in the chinks.

The dragon turned around, not wanting escape but revenge.

The dragon inhaled and shuddered, and it seemed like the dragon was going to break, but she exhaled and blew a column of flames so bright that I couldn't even watch.

Sarah dodged the blast, but it hit her mother full force.

"NO!" Sarah screamed. She fired her own blast at the dragon, and she stopped and fled.

"Mom!"

"I'm fine… honey, but I'm weak… I'll go with you…"

"NO!"

I promise that I won't leave you… again… I'm coming with you."

"Don't…" Sarah said. Tears streaked down her cheeks. She rushed away on her flame hover board after the dragon.

"Hey!" she yelled at the dragon. "Stop being a coward and fight!" The dragon turned around and growled.

"Yeah dummy! Stand and fight!" And the dragon charged.

…

The first part of the fight went really well.

Sarah dodged the dragon's charge and grabbed hold of her tail. Sarah yanked back, and the dragon roared. I looked at her hands, and they were cut, scratched and bleeding.

The dragon started flying, and Sarah started getting dragged along.

"Nooo!" she screamed. She tried to release her hands, but the dragon threw her down onto the ground. She summoned a barrier of fire, but the dragon just plowed her head through it. She lashed out a massive hand and grabbed Sarah by the neck. Sarah closed her eyes. I was thinking: This is the end. This is the end.

The dragon opened up her other claw to slash Sarah.

She sliced downwards. Suddenly, a blast of flames disoriented the dragon, and he released his grip.

"Mom!" Sarah yelled. She got back up and charged into battle. Sarah, with her mom, got the dragon pinned down. Suddenly, time froze. Yharon appeared in an explosion of flames.

"You know you can't kill him," he growled. "You've slowed me down too much." He disappeared, and a trail of fire sprang from where he was to the dragon.

Suddenly, she had a burst of energy.

She fired a tiny whirlwind of flames.

Sarah ignored it, but when it hit the ground and burst, it swirled into a massive fire tornado that was even bigger than the dragon.

Sarah grabbed onto a boulder in the ground, but her mom wasn't as lucky. She got sucked into the swirling vortex of flames.

"MOM!" Sarah cried. She let go of the rock and flew toward the tornado.

Inside, it was almost impossible to see. The flames spinning around made me dizzy and confused. Sarah saw her mom and rushed toward help, but she kept getting pulled back

"Are you okay?" Sarah screamed, but her voice was drowned out by the spinning whirlwind.

The dragon appeared through the flames and tried to get to Sarah, but this time the tornado actually helped. She was pulled around, straight to her mom. Sarah used all her might to drag her mom out of the tornado, but she didn't have to. The tornado died down, and the dragon fled, leaving

Sarah, crouched over her mom, who lying as still as stone.

...

We went out of the vision. Sarah's mom was gone.

"What was..." I looked at Selena, Zach, and Sarah to see if they had experienced the same thing. They definitely did.

Sarah sat down on the sidewalk, her face buried in her hands.

"I'm so sorry. Sarah..." Selena tried to comfort her.

"It's okay," Sarah murmured. "Now you know why we came here. I'm sorry I wasted your time..."

"Wasted?" I said. "This isn't a waste of time. I'm so sorry Sarah."

"Should we... um-" Zach grunted.

"No, I'm fine." Sarah took a deep breath. "Ever since, I could only use little blasts of fire magic at a time. I used up all my energy in that... battle. That's why I passed out at the Arch."

"Let's go to the Liberty Bell. It radiates peace, so no monsters can go near it." Selena suggested.

"Okay. Anything but monsters," I said. I looked around and saw that there were a few tall kids walking to us.

"Hey, punk," the leader yelled. Selena reached into her pocket. Her pocket? I thought. Then I realized that the wind blade was probably magic and could shrink.

"You got some money?" one of the kids growled.

"No." Selena really looked like she wanted to draw her sword. The kids advanced.

"Run," I whispered. And that's what we did.

…

We always pick the wrong shop to hide in.

This time, we were in some kind of department store, filled to the brim with rows and rows of ugly sweaters and plump cushions.

"May I help you?" a man behind the counter asked. I gasped. He looked like the opposite of Yharon, but he had the same aura of power. He wore a pale, white blazer over a white shirt, and he wore misty, dull, purple pants. The only thing that made him look different was that he wore tinted glasses, and had a bulky ski cap on.

"Um.. yeah! We'd like to try on some… um sweaters." I managed.

"Oh! Sweaters? Why would you want sweaters?" the man asked. "It's summer now." I looked at his name tag. It read Yarin. Although Yarin was a real name, it still was awfully close to Yharon.

"Um… because we want to go on a ski trip," Zach offered.

"In the middle of the summer? Okay then. Sit down." He patted a couch that was next to him. I whispered to Selena, "Trust him?"

"No…" We all cautiously sat down. Zach's cushion seemed especially squishy. He even started sinking in.

"So…" Yarin said. "What kind of sweaters? Do you-"

"Is this couch safe?" Zach muttered. He patted the leather covering.

"Wait...what?" Sarah said.

"Oh, that's nothing. Let me get some jackets for you to try on." He walked off to a room.

"Uh… guys?" Zach said. "I'm stuck."

"What?" I exclaimed.

"The couch's pulling you in!" Selena said.

"Oh no… Just push up! Push up!" We all came over and tried to help Zach out, but we couldn't do anything.

"I can cut him free!" I yelled, but I heard Yarin coming over.

"Push him over," I said, and we rolled him behind a cabinet so that Yarin wouldn't be suspicious.

"Where's the other one?" Yarin asked innocently.

"Bathroom," I quickly said.

"Okay… Here are some sweaters for you. For, you, young lady, we have this." He brought out the most hideous jacket ever. It was bright pink, and had hearts and sprinkles all over it.

"Um, thanks…" she muttered. I tried not to laugh, and Selena glared at me.

"I also brought a pair of shoes, because we have a special deal these few days. Here, young gentleman. Come try these on." I probably shouldn't have laughed, because these shoes were even worse. They were bright neon and had purple shoelaces. There was glitter on the shoes, so they sparkled whichever way you turned them.

Selena unfolded her jacket and I put on my new flashy pair of shoes at the same time.

"Great!" Yarin grinned and snapped his fingers. Right after he did that, I felt my new shoes tighten.

"What… Whoa!" The shoes seemed to bond together, and I tripped and fell on the ground. Yarin clapped his hands together once, and tendrils of thick rope bound me. I looked at Selena, and she didn't look any better. The sweater seemed to have glued itself together. Her hands were bound.

Sarah jumped up to help, but Yarin snapped his fingers again, and ropes leaped from the couch and tied her down.

"Who are you?" Sarah yelled.

"Me?" Yarin said calmly. "I'm Yharon's brother, Alluvion." He pulled off his cap and his glasses. He looked almost exactly like Yharon, except that his eyes were misty and light, and his hair was like a shadowy cloud. "Or to be exact, I'm his twin." He suddenly transformed into a blinding gray light. He now looked a whole lot more powerful.

"I just wanted to get you tied up, so you listen up." Alluvion looked straight at me. "I might be your only chance of survival against Abaddon."

…

Everything went pretty smoothly, in my opinion, except that Zach came and charged in.

"Ahhhhh!" Zach screamed, wielding a club. He tripped over a shoe rack, spilling multicolored flip-flops everywhere, and tried to blast Alluvion with green magic, but ropes came up and entangled him.

"Okay." Alluvion nodded. "We're ready to talk."

"So first," I interrupted. "What's your story?"

"Well, as I said, I am Alluvion. We were born as twins, but of course, Yharon was the older one. By two seconds, I think." He pouted like a little boy, and then continued his story. "So he became king of the world, of course. So I went down here to work at a department store! I've been wanting to get revenge on him ever since, so I can help you!"

"Uh… Can you untie us first?" Sarah asked.

"No."

"Why?"

"Because I want to make sure that you don't revolt against me!"

"We won't," I pleaded. "Please. We want to defeat Abaddon and Yharon too!"

"Oh!" Alluvion exclaimed. "Let's get out of this shop first. Time is different in here." He untied our bonds, and we walked outside. It was a bright new day.

"What's… what's the date?" Sarah gasped.

"The date? Hmm… It's the fourteenth."

"Oh no," Selena murmured. There was only one day until the Corruption spread to the borders of Fort Azari.

…

"So," Alluvion grinned. "Sit down."

"Where?" I asked.

"Here." He gestured to open air, but suddenly, a couch and some benches appeared.

"Is it trapped?"

"Why, never!" He sat down on a bench and showed us.

"Ok…" Selena muttered. We all sat down.

"How can you help us?" Zach demanded. "We're already late!"

"Well, I can only help you at the right time. For now, you'll be on your own."

"Really!" Selena shouted angrily. "You waste a night and all we get is no help? Really?"

"Silence, child," Alluvion ordered, and Selena's mouth snapped shut. "You know you can't battle against me. It would be better to follow me. Take all the help you can get."

"Ok…" I said. Suddenly, Alluvion frowned.

"Someone approaches," he said. "Leave at once." He snapped his fingers, and Selena's mouth opened again.

"Sarah, taxi!" I yelled. We sprinted away, and I saw someone creep up behind Alluvion. This was an explosion of darkness, and Alluvion summoned mist to cover the area. I didn't see who the person was, but was sure of whom it was. Abaddon.

Chapter 6

A few minutes later, we were cruising comfortably in another Tesla Model X. Thanks again, Sarah!

"Better get some sleep," I encouraged. "I also think that Alluvion opened up dreams for us again, so hopefully, we'll be getting some soon."

"Yeah." Selena agreed.

"It'll be about ninety to one hundred miles to New York, but we have until midnight, so no rush." Zach announced.

"Okay." Selena and I said in unison. We all laughed.

"Sleep tight people because there might not even be a world left to sleep in tomorrow," I said, and I closed my eyes. Selena, still in the back with me, leaned her head against me, and I smiled.

"Sleep tight," I murmured, and dreams took me once again.

...

I saw Alluvion and Abaddon clashing against each other. There still was a blanket of mist in the area, but I could see through it clearly now. Abaddon launched shadow blasts and summoned shades to fight for him, but he was having a hard

93

time. Coils of pale blue rope were tripping him and pulling him down. Alluvion was firing blasts of mist and sparkles that seemed to confuse Abaddon.

Suddenly, Abaddon launched over Alluvion and summoned a dark dagger. He brought it down onto the god's back, suddenly; he disappeared and reappeared on a building.

Abaddon roared and sent a tremor that caused the whole building to collapse. Alluvion teleported again, and waved his hand, causing another blanket of mist to cover the area. Abaddon leaped from the ground, but the sun made his form flicker.

Alluvion closed his eyes and let out a mighty yell that shattered even my dream. He collapsed on the ground.

As the dream faded, I saw deadly spikes rain from the sky and impale them into the concrete. Abaddon maneuvered all of them, trying to get to Alluvion. Just as he thought that the spike rain was over, a massive one fell from the sky and struck Abaddon in the back. He screamed in pain and yelled: "I'll get you!" and he faded away in the shadows.

...

Another dream? I thought. I saw Abaddon's castle up close, and Randy was sprawled on the ground, not moving.

"Too… dark…" he moaned. "Can't… stop…"
Oh no! I thought. We have to hurry. The dream
changed again.

…

Abaddon was limping through a dense
rainforest. I saw Yharon's castle up ahead.

"Your brother is too strong at day…" Abaddon
groaned when he got to Yharon, who was waiting in
the fiery garden.

"Really?" he mused. "Too strong? Oh well.
You'll be better by sundown, I hope. Also, check on
the dragon."

"Yes, sir…" Abaddon said, and he hobbled
away into the palace.

"Too weak…" Yharon muttered, shaking his
head. A thick magical fog flowed into the garden.

"ALLUVION!" Yharon screamed into the mist.
"YOU HAVE BETRAYED ME, AND YOU WILL
PAY!" Yharon raised his hands, crackling with
solar energy, and unleashed a searing white bolt of
flame, so deadly that even I could feel the power
pulsing from the bolt. The fog kept on building up
and combusting with the flame. Suddenly, there was
an enormous explosion. My dream shattered again,
and I jolted awake.

…

I took a deep breath. Alluvion was still okay. We were fine. Except I don't think Selena appreciated it.

"What... was... that?" she yawned. "Next time, I won't use you as a cushion."

"Well, I had a dream again." I said.

"Okay..."

"Well, Alluvion is safe, so I think we'll be okay."

"That's good. So we might have reinforcements if we need it." Selena said. "Will, I have to confess something."

"Okay."

"I've been having dreams too," Selena muttered.

"What were they?" I asked.

"Well, once, I was in Aer's palace in the sky. She...well, she said that Abaddon wouldn't stop the Corruption unless we got the other legendary weapon. I didn't want to worry you guys even more..."

"It's okay. Let's just focus on this thing right now."

"Okay then."

"It'll be fine," I said. "So are you ready for today? It's sunny today, and I don't know if that's a good thing."

"Yeah." Selena took a deep breath and smiled. "I'm ready."

...

"Where do you want to go?" I asked. "Sundown's about eight thirty today, so we got plenty of time to search around."

"Umm..." Selena cleared her throat. "Confession time, my dad lives here. I want to visit him. That's another reason, I wanted to come on the mission, but of course, I wanted to save the world, right?"

"Ok. That's fine with us" said Sarah. "Where does your father live?"

"Oh! In an apartment a few blocks from the Empire State Building."

...

My nerves felt jumpy as we approached our destination. I wondered how Selena's dad was. While we were walking, I asked her about him.

"So, how's your dad like? Is he nice?" Selena looked away, and I knew that I hit a bad spot

"Oh. Sorry."

"No, I should tell you. He's a lawyer, so he's really busy all the time. When I was born, he sort of ignored me, so I ran away from home. Aer brought me to Fort Azari, and here I am. I've sent a few letters to him over the years, but I've not talked to him much."

"Then why do you want to visit him?" I wondered.

"Well, I want to get better with him again. I really want him to move back to San Diego or Los Angeles, because there are too many monsters around here. But I just want to... talk to him. I haven't seen him since I've run away."

"Okay." I answered. "Well, we have a whole day to do it, so no rush."

"Thanks." When we walked to Selena's apartment, there were so many enemies milling around. I saw a whole motorcycle gang of shadow ghouls, and in a church we saw a band of necromancers, chanting some kind of ritual around a pedestal. Then, the pedestal blew up, and all their heads fell off.

The only trouble we had was when a new monster that I had never met, a spiritualist. It started when I saw a tiny blue cloud made of glittering dust that was following us. I thought that Alluvion had sent some kind of tracer after us to watch us.

Suddenly, my back exploded in pain.

"Ahh!" I wailed. White spots danced before my eyes.

"What?" Selena yelled.

"A spiritualist!" Zach screamed.

"Where?" Sarah said.

"Don't know! Could be anywhere..." Selena said. I managed to get up, and I drew Malachite and tried to slash at the spirit.

"Don't!" Zach yelled. But I couldn't stop. The spirit exploded into dust and reformed, summoning two tiny blue ghosts that charged me. I sliced them in half.

"What do I do?" I groaned. Suddenly, I saw a flash of white in the corner of my eye.

"There's the spirit- whatever it's called!" I called. I crawled away from the spirit and turned to face the spiritualist. I was not ready for this experience.

She had a white, flowing cloak with a bluish tint, and she had a timeless, beautiful, pale face. She was holding a staff with a blue ghost on top of it. I completely forgot everything, the pain, my friends, and turned to face her.

"Come to me," she whispered.

"NO! Will, don't!" Selena shouted. I lost focus for a second, and I felt the spirit eating into my back. I turned and again the spiritualist said: "Come William." That put me out of focus. Rarely anyone called me William, and I realized that she wanted to kill me. I drew Malachite and lunged.

The sword elongated and stuck her in the chest. A couple of spirits exploded out of her as she disappeared. They all crowded around me like they were hugging me.

"What's this?" I said.

"They're following you. Like my dogs, they're yours now." Selena answered. I wanted to enjoy having minions, but suddenly someone grabbed my shoulder. I turned and saw a big and buff police officer.

"Hey," he growled. "It's illegal to stab someone like that."

"Run!" I screamed. Sarah grabbed the staff that the spiritualist was holding.

"Stop there!" the old lady yelled. Suddenly, I lifted off the ground in my attempt to get away, and in a sudden burst of speed, I blasted forward. I turned and saw Selena straining to push all of us forward.

We were far, far away from the mob, and we slowed down.

"Oh, my… gosh…" Selena took a deep breath. Sarah held up the staff.

"Who wants it?" she said.

"Can I?" Zach asked, panting. "I don't have an actual weapon that looks cool." He looked around for agreement, and we all nodded.

"Catch!" Sarah said. She tossed the staff at Zach, who fumbled with it for a second and then dropped it on the ground.

"We're almost there," Selena pointed out, looking at the Empire State Building.

"What the…" Sarah gasped in awe. Suddenly, a huge chunk of dark stone flickered into view. It was linked by a skinny wooden bridge, and across it was an assortment of buildings, walls, and towers.

"Abaddon's fortress," Zach murmured.

"There's my dad's apartment," Selena said, pointing to the left.

"Okay," I said. "Let's go."

. . .

"Ready?" Zach said nervously to Selena.

"Ready as could be."

"Go." I urged her. She took a deep breath and knocked on the doorbell.

"Coming!" a deep voice boomed. Selena closed her eyes and took another deep breath. The door opened, and Selena's father stepped out.

"Who…" he muttered, on the phone. Then he abruptly stopped, and his face lightened. "Call me back later, okay?" He hung up. I tried to think about how he resembled, but I couldn't Selena. He had a mop of jet black hair and had a bushy mustache. Just like any lawyer (at least of what I know), he wore an expensive blazer and dress clothing.

"Dear! You're back!" he said, and ran forward and hugged Selena.

"Dad…" She didn't talk anymore, because she was sobbing in his shirt. I felt a bit uncomfortable just standing there, so I peeked into the room.

It was really orderly in the apartment. There was a living room with a few couches and a flat screen T.V. to the left, there was a hallway that led to a bedroom and a bathroom and after the living room, there was a kitchen with a refrigerator. Her dad let us into the apartment, and we sat down on the couches.

"We're friends of Selena," I said. "I'm Will, and these are Sarah and Zach."

"Hello, Mr. um…" Sarah grunted.

"Oh! Call me Mr. Mayne." Selena released her dad and plopped down next to me. She was still sniffling, so she grabbed a wad of tissues. Mr. Mayne's phone rang again, and he picked it up.

"I'm really sorry, dear," he whispered. "I just need to finish this phone call, and I'll be right with you. I love you, dear. Go into your old bedroom and make yourselves at home.

We headed into the room, where I dumped my backpack onto the bed and lay down on the carpet. There was a table with books and papers stacked high on it, and there was a cabinet with a mirror next to the bed. I looked at the clock on the wall and it read one o'clock.

"We still have time." I said, but I felt the tension growing. Suddenly, the apartment didn't feel as friendly now.

"That's good," Zach said.

"Selena," Sarah said. "Your dad seemed really friendly, how-"

"Didn't you see?" She shook her head. "He's better now, but he's on a phone call half of the day! And also, back then, he just thought that I was an annoyance. But…" Her voice died down. "Sorry."

"Ok," Sarah responded. "That's okay. Now, will, we need to check on that wound in your back. I lied on my stomach, and Zach gasped. The apartment really didn't seem friendly now. In fact, white spots were dancing around my eyes. My vision waned.

"Oh no," I muttered. "Is it the spirits?" I asked, looking at the pale blue wisps fluttering around.

"Yes," Selena said gravely. "It's almost gotten to your soul."

The wound looked terrible. There was a hole in the back of my shirt, and it was sparking with blue light.

"Why doesn't it hurt?" I muttered.

"The pain's probably so unbearable that you don't feel it," Selena answered hastily. "Give me your spell tome." I handed it over, and as I did, I doubled over in pain. I grabbed onto Selena's shoulder and collapsed.

"I'm guessing that you don't heal these things like regular wounds, right?" Sarah asked. "Because I want to be a doctor when I grow up, and I don't think a doctor would help here."

"There's still healing power radiating from this!" Zach exclaimed. "It's been keeping you alive, Will."

"Come on, come on!" Selena muttered, flipping through the pages. Red spots danced before my eyes.

"Found it!" she yelled triumphantly. She started chanting words, but she was too slow. My eyes closed, and I felt Selena's hands against my back, channeling power into my body.

Suddenly, I slipped into another vision, this time with Selena at my side.

...

"Where are we?" Selena wondered. There was a floating castle made of white stones up ahead, and we were floating toward it.

"My back is better," I noted, feeling my shirt.

"That's good," Selena said. Suddenly, she gasped. "This... this is Aer's palace!"

"Wow," I said. "It's so beautiful." We touched down on the ground, and we walked forward through the main gates. There was a garden to the right, and I saw Aer.

Now I saw family resemblance. Aer had brown hair like Selena, and she was also really beautiful. Even though she looked perfect, I just liked Selena without all the glamorous clothes. She wore a blue sleeveless dress that flowed like the wind, and she seemed to be floating around instead of walking.

"Come," she said, quietly. We walked forward. Aer summoned some chairs beckoned for us to sit down.

"I have come to send you a message." she smiled. "You must trust yourself, Selena. When the time comes, you must believe. You will know what it is, but do not lose hope. I send you off with my blessing. Your wound will be healed when you come back, William." The palace faded away.

...

Time unfroze again, and I felt perfectly normal. I looked at Selena, at by her face, I could tell that she was in the vision too.

"Guys," I said. "We had a vision."

"What? You're fine again?" Zach asked incredulously. "I guess Sarah's actually a good doctor!" We told Sarah and Zach about the vision.

"That's good," Sarah said. "We can have some confidence that Selena will save us now!"

"Um… No." Selena grunted. "I have no idea what she was talking about."

"You'll figure it out," I promised.

"Selena dear!" Mr. Mayne called.

"Okay," Selena said. "I'll go talk him now. You guys stay in the room, okay?"

"Sure," Sarah answered. Selena left the room.

"Rest up guys," Zach announced. "Long night ahead," I closed my eyes, wanting to just sleep for fifteen minutes, hoping for no dream. Unfortunately, it came again.

…

I was somewhere in Yharon's palace, in some cages. I saw Yharon's dragon in one of the cages, thrashing and roaring. Someone, or something, was feeding her some kind of food.

The room looked like any old room in Yharon's palace. Red carpeted floors, chandeliers, and ceilings so high you couldn't see the top.

But something was different about the room. The walls were stone, and it felt like I was underground.

"Betsy's almost ready," the monster feeding the dragon food growled to himself. He turned, and I saw him.

He had a regular human face, but his eyes were yellow flames. He held a flaming pike in one hand, and in the other, he held a box labeled Betsy Food. He wore red armor and leggings, and his hair was a mess of flames. Yharon stepped into the room.

"Good," he said. "While you're at it, polish my golf shoes. I got an invitation to play in Palm Springs, and I want to look good!"

"Yes sir," Yharon nodded and left the room. Suddenly, a fine blue mist seeped through the open doorway.

"What?" the monster snarled. "Wha- what's this? I-" He coughed and choked, and when the fog cleared, there was a pile of armor and a spear.

Betsy didn't seem harmed though, which sort of sucked. Then, my dream dissolved.

...

"What's the time?" I yawned, and I looked at the clock, five in the afternoon. Selena was sleeping quietly next to me. I stood up and snuck out of the room.

Sarah and Zach were crashed on the couches in the living room, eating nachos. Yum, I thought. Sarah turned around. "Go take a shower, Will. You look terrible."

"Okay," I responded, and left for the bathroom.

When I came out of the bathroom, Selena was awake.

"Hi," I said.

"Your hair's a mess," Selena responded. Yeah. That's how I get greeted by my friends.

"So what'd you talk about with your dad?"

"He actually knows about the gods and stuff, and also about Fort Azari. But I said that I wanted to come back over the school year and live with him."

"That's good," I said. Selena nodded.

"Well," I said. "Meet you on the couch with nachos!"

"There's nachos?"

"Yeah."

"Okay! I might not take a shower anymore."

...

"Why are you watching the news?" I demanded. "We should be preparing for battle... Can I have some nachos?"

"Wait," Sarah said, stopping me from changing the channel. "Look at this."

"Massive storm is gathering at Los Angeles. We've got all of the people evacuated, but we're still not sure of what it is." The camera showed a picture of dark, shadowy, purple clouds.

"Oh no." I murmured.

"Next up," the reporter announced. "Will Hanson and his case. Who is he? Stay tuned as we head into a short commercial break."

"Can I change the channel now?" I muttered angrily.

"Shouldn't we show Selena though?" Zach suggested.

"Show me what?" Selena asked, stepping out of the bathroom.

"Your hair is even more of a mess," I grunted. Zach looked at me for approval, and I nodded.

"Go ahead," I said. "Selena, I'm on T.V. Yay." Selena gasped at what the camera's recording showed. I was holding some kind of knife, and I was stabbing a young girl.

"Great recorder," I grumbled. "I'm switching now." I grabbed the remote and switched the channel, but it appeared as the Weather Channel.

"Oh my god," I groaned, as the person on the screen talked about the weird clouds gathering in Los Angeles.

"-also expected to be a solar eclipse in Los Angeles." Selena jolted up.

"What? That's the time when Abaddon's the strongest. No!"

"Well, there's nothing we can do about that," Sarah groaned. "But keep positive, although we're about to die, probably."

"Yeah, positive!" I grinned. "Have some nachos, Selena!"

Chapter 7

"Well," Mr. Mayne said. "You better be on your way," make sure you come back, Selena." He kissed her on the forehead and smiled.

"Bye dad!" Selena called. When she looked away, there were tears in her eyes.

"Let's go kick some monsters," I said.

…

Getting to the observatory deck on the Empire State Building was easy. Crossing the bridge was not.

"Is this safe?" I wondered.

"Should be," Zach grunted. "If other dumb monsters can cross, why can't we?"

"Remember," Selena reminded us. "Stealth mission," She got it easy to cross. She just flew straight across the air and landed on the other side.

"No traps or anything!" she called from the island.

"How do we cross?" I yelled.

"The bridge, dummy!" she answered back.

"Okay, then. If you say so…" I put one foot on the bridge, and then another. The other people on the place completely ignored us. My heart was pounding inside my chest. In one sudden burst of speed, I made it across.

"You made it!"

"Of course Airhead, What do you think?" Zach crossed next. Or, he actually didn't cross. He turned into a falcon and flew across.

"Can you go scout ahead?" I asked the bird. Zach cawed in response. I hoped that meant Sure! and not something else. He flew off.

Now only Sarah was left.

"You can do it!" I cheered.

"Umm…" Her hair burst into flames, and she swatted it out.

"You're halfway!" I yelled. Suddenly, her foot exploded in fire, and the bridge smoldered.

"Almost there," Sarah murmured. She made the flames go out, but the bridge didn't like it.

"Run!" Selena screamed, and Sarah started sprinting. Then the bridge gave way.

"No!" I yelled and reached down to grab Sarah. Of course, there was no way that I was strong enough to hold onto her, so when I grabbed her hand, I toppled of the edge. Another hand grabbed me. I looked up and saw Selena using to winds to try to force us up. Her hair was flying back and smacking her face and eyes, but we kept pulling and straining.

Just as I thought that I would snap in two, someone, or something else pulled us pack up.

"Thanks!" I said, and turned face to face with an elephant.

"Eeeep!" I yelped, and nearly fell off the edge again, but the giant beast morphed back into Zach.

"Oh, sorry," I muttered, looking down.

"Did you see anything?" Selena asked.

"Yeah," Zach answered. Judging from the look on his face, there was something really bad. "There are swarms of enemies in the streets. Shadow ghouls, necromancers, even some more spiritualists. We might need the sun spell activated all the time, so I stole this." He held up a rusty lantern and flicked his finger.

A single spark flew from his hand and into the lantern.

"An Eternal Flame!" Selena gasped. "Where'd you find that? They're really powerful." The lantern grew brighter and brighter until Zach dropped it.

"Hot, hot, hot, hot, hot!" He shook his hand out. "Sarah, you take it…" The flames enveloped the lantern itself until just became a glowing yellow ball that made the area around us look like day.

"And to answer your question, Selena," Zach said. "I stole it from a sun guard. Who knows what he's doing here. And who knows why he has it in the first place."

"Ready?" I asked.

"No," Sarah admitted.

"Let's go." I said, and we sprinted off.

…

I'm pretty sure that Zach underestimated the number of monsters. Everywhere I looked down the dark, jagged buildings; there were monsters upon monsters upon monsters. Zach pointed in one direction and said, "I traced a route to Abaddon's palace. We first go down that way, toward the mountain."

I peered upward and saw the tall, shadowy tower on top of the huge mountain.

"Here we go," I said, and we charged.

I blasted a group of shadow ghouls with elemental magic while my spirits and Selena's dogs headed over to three necromancers. I swung Malachite, and beams of blue light appeared and flew over to some spiritualists and sliced them.

Selena slashed and hacked through hordes of enemies with her wind blade, and occasionally released bursts of wind and tiny tornados.

Zach was helping a lot. His spirit staff was keeping the spiritualists from reaching into our souls, and he whacked monsters on the head and blasted them with crackling green energy.

Sarah summoned two fire daggers and was mowing down rows and rows of enemies. Very rarely, she would unleash an outburst of flames, and a few monsters would become toast.

The whole battle scene looked amazing, and I wish I had time to enjoy it. There were shadowy beams and abyss balls going everywhere, and blasts of green light radiated in the air. Flames leaped high, and little balls of mist, spirits, were leeching onto the monsters and eating them. Malachite's beams were annihilating some shadow ghouls, and the eternal ball of fire illuminated the whole area.

Finally, after the last bit of monster was reduced to dust, we stopped.

"Wow..." Sarah gasped, looking at the destruction all around her.

"We need to hurry though," Selena pointed out. "Time is running out." She pointed at the moon that was slowly making its way to its peak.

"I took a watch," Sarah said. "It's still nine. Three hours. No prob."

"Okay..." Zach muttered. We forged ahead.

"Now turn left," he said. "The main gate's that way."

"But shouldn't we climb the mountain?" Selena suggested. "It would bring us directly to the throne room."

"But you're the good climber," I grumbled. Suddenly, there was a loud roar from the main gates. I gulped. "Maybe the mountain is better." We started to climb the steep, treacherous hill.

. . .

When we were a quarter ways up the hill, I forced myself to look back. Then I saw the monster.

It had bony pale white skin that was studded with shadowy spikes. Its four claws had spikes on them that were made for climbing up mountains.

It breathed purple flames at us, but when it couldn't reach us, it started climbing.

"Go spirits!" I yelled, and they engaged in battle. I knew that the monster would claw through them, but they still slowed it down.

Selena, above, found a relatively flat place to stop. Everyone else got up, so she grabbed my hands and hauled me up.

"That's enough climbing for a day," I groaned. I drew Malachite fired some beams at the monster, but they barely did anything. The ball of flame that Sarah had was attracting all the monsters camped around Abaddon's palace. Soon, we would be surrounded.

"Target the drakon's crystals!" Zach yelled. Sarah unleashes the Eternal Flame, and the drakon backed off a bit.

Below, the monsters cheered the drakon on because they couldn't climb the steep slope. The drakon whipped its tail, and three shadow blasts rained down on us. Luckily, we dodged all of them, but the area we were on started to crumble.

The necromancers formed ranks and opened their spell tomes. I drew mine out and whispered a protection spell. A huge array of shadow blasts came lying straight at us, and the invisible barrier shattered.

"Climb!" Selena encouraged, and I continued heading up. The drakon blew purple flames again, and the rocks melted wherever they touched. The ground vibrated from underneath us.

"I don't think that this is stable," I muttered. Suddenly, another barrage of spells was launched by the necromancers. This time, it was an assortment of spells. A bunch of toxic fumes appeared and exploded when a few fireballs landed near them. This weakened the mountain even more, and it started to cave in.

"GO!" Selena screamed. The rocks above us started tumbling down and smashing into the monsters below, narrowly missing us. The monsters realized that they were causing landslides, so the necromancers switched back to firing shadow bolts at us.

We found another flat area on the mountain to stop at.

"We're half way!" Zach said, and then yelped as a shadow ball flew past him.

"Spirits go to the necromancers!" I yelled, and they slowly floated downward.

The drakon roared and tried to get to us, but there was a flat wall that was made by the necromancers blocking its path.

"Keep going while the drakon's stuck down there," Sarah said. Selena blew a funnel of air down at the beast, and it fell down even farther.

I don't think that it was a good thing, because the fall caused a tremor that created a crack between the earth. I tumbled down one side and barely caught hold of the cliff.

"Will!" Selena rushed forward. Zach transformed into a leopard (not a grizzly bears again, luckily, because it might have caused the mountain to collapse) and sprinted forward and almost ran off the cliff.

Selena grabbed my hand and hauled me up with the strength of Zach.

"Two times already," I muttered. "I almost fall off a cliff, and I get saved. At some point, I'll fall."

"You're welcome," Selena grinned. The crack spread even farther, and Sarah was on the other side.

"Jump!" I yelled at her.

"I- I- can't!" Sarah trembled.

"You can do it!" Selena yelled. "But hurry!" Sarah took a deep breath and charged forward. She leaped. I ran forward just in case she fell again, but she made it.

Suddenly, the rocks shifted and closed up the gap again.

"I could have just done that!" Sarah complained.

"Oh well..." I muttered. Suddenly, a huge shadow loomed above us. The drakon had managed to get above us.

It lunged into battle. Selena's two dogs ferociously attacked the monster, but they were barely doing anything. Selena used the winds to funnel it away, and that was keeping it just at bay.

I leaped onto its body and slashed at the shadow spikes studded all over it. The drakon roared and whipped its giant tail. I felt a stinging pain in my back, and I forced myself to turn around.

The drakon's tail was stuck in my back. I yanked it out and almost fell off his back.

Below, the necromancers attacked again. Another shadow beam blast came flying, and they all missed except for one, which drilled into my shoulder. I cried out in pain and fell off the drakon.

"Will!" Selena screamed, and I tumbled down the mountain.

The monsters cheered from below and rubbed their hands together.

I stopped myself from falling any further about two-fifths of the way down.

"Ouch," I groaned. I looked up and saw Selena and Sarah battling the drakon. Zach was nowhere to be seen, but sometimes one of the spikes on the beast would chip off, and I knew that Zach was up to something.

I tried climbing up the mountain again, but my left arm ringed with pain. I took out my spell tome and whispered the healing spell. I felt my arm grow stronger again, but I still was too weak to climb back up. The blasts of shadow were growing stronger at the moment, and I looked up at the moon. It was going too quick.

Suddenly, there was a huge explosion from above, and the drakon went flying. Rocks came tumbling down, and I tried to move to dodge all of them. Suddenly, a large boulder smashed my head, and I went unconscious.

...

"Am... am I dead?" I moaned. I saw a ghostly face hovering above me.

"Alluvion?"

"Yes. I thought that this would be the best time to give you some information. You're not dead. You're being tended by your friends right now. But make sure that you don't lose hope. I'm still a bit harmed here, so I might be a bit late to your aid."

"Okay. Any help is fine here."

"Good. I'll be sending you off to your island. Also, beware of the trap."

"What trap?" But my dream faded away.

...

"Ow," I groaned.

"You're awake!" Zach grinned. "Selena, your healing worked!"

"Good," she said and then smiled at me. "I'm so glad you're alive, Will. While I was healing you, I made a nickname for you! I'll tell you after this is done."

"Oh no," I muttered.

"Guys," Sarah said. "We have two hours to do this. We gotta hurry now."

"How far up are we?" I asked.

"We reached the top of the mountain, but we have a problem." Selena responded. She pointed at the large tower looming above us. "We need to enter the castle anyway." There was a small lookout area that we could go into.

"Through there?" I said.

"Yeah…" Zach answered.

"Well, what are you guys waiting for? Let's go!"

We jumped over the railing easily. But the castle was an absolute nightmare. When we were in there, we had no idea where to go. Once we entered, we could either go left or right.

"Go left," Sarah suggested. "That's the way to the tower."

"Okay." We walked that way, the eternal light casting a bright glow around the area. Once we got in, the hallway behind us seemed to dissolve.

"Uh…" I muttered. "I think we're horribly lost." We ran into a corridor that led three different directions.

"Forward, right?" Selena suggested.

"Uh," Zach said. "There is no forward."

"What? Where…" I turned around, confused. "Which way is forward?"

"I see why the monsters didn't want to go in here," Sarah muttered.

"I can use the air," Selena suggested. Because we didn't have anything else to do, we agreed.

"That way," Selena pointed to one corridor. We walked down that way. "And now… umm… through there," She pointed to a hallway that was marked off with two large columns.

"Okay…" I grumbled. "Wish I had that power too…" We came out into a large circular tower that had a spiral staircase in the middle.

"We're here!" Zach exclaimed, and rushed toward the stairs.

"No!" I yelled. "The tower is too narrow. It's a trap. We gotta go that way. I pointed to another hallway. We forged ahead, and made many weird turns, but we finally made it to a huge corridor. We walked forward and saw that there was a smaller central staircase.

"Here we are," Selena and I said at the same time. We turned and smiled at each other. We tramped up the spiral staircase.

"I don't think that we were very sneaky, though," I said.

"Sneaky enough," Selena answered. We finally made it to the top. We came into the throne room that I had seen so many times in my dreams.

"Randy!" Zach yelled, and rushed forward to help him. Randy opened his eyes as he saw the light.

"Will! Selena! What are you doing here? Where am... oh!"

"You were going insane, Randy." I explained to him my dreams.

"Well, that's not good." Randy responded. "Let's hope that doesn't happen to me."

"Should I cut you free?" I asked him.

"Please do." I drew Malachite and sliced the metal chains from his hands and feet.

"Are you okay?" I asked Randy.

"Maybe. I'll have to rest up. I probably can't use any water magic for a long time, because the shadows have drained my powers."

"Okay. We need to get the Key of Nightmares now." I rushed to the throne, and Selena followed close behind. Zach and Sarah tended to Randy. I looked at the throne. Etched carefully on it was the shape of a key. I touched it. There was a tiny beeping sound, but nothing happened.

"Look at the back," I suggested. Selena went around and cried: "I found it!" She pulled out a key from the back of the throne.

"Awesome," I said. "But don't you think that this was a little too easy? No guards in here or anything?" Suddenly, Selena paled.

"Too easy?" a voice growled behind us. My blood turned ice cold. "Why, we would never make anything too easy."

I turned around and saw a cloaked figure, about seven feet tall. I couldn't see his face, but I could see glowing purple eyes behind the shadows. He held a long rod that had a writhing ball of shadows on top of it.

"We wouldn't let you go," he said. "But I would be interested to see you try…" I knew who this was.

"Signus," I muttered. "You're the one who's been following me the whole time. You were watching me."

"Oh!" he said. "Don't get too mad now, dears."

This was the trap.

Chapter 8

"How…" I gasped.

"I've been following you the whole time, dears." Signus answered. "But when you got across the bridge, I returned to Abaddon's castle. And here I am. You've done pretty well, but you've just gone a bit overboard." He prepared to attack.

"The flame!" Selena shouted. "Give it to Will!"

"Okay!" Sarah yelled back. A ball of flames leaped over Signus' head, and I caught it. I thought that it would burn me, but it only felt warm in my hand.

I tried willing it to float above my head, and it did.

"Go," I said to Selena, and we leaped into battle.

The Eternal Flame shot tendrils of flame that hit Signus. He blocked most of them with his staff, but still one got through and zapped him. He cried out in pain, but it was more like a bug bite than a real wound.

We leaped forward, and I drew Malachite. Selena took out her wind blade. Although now two people were attacking, he still easily evaded all our attacks. He shot balls of shadow that exploded into raging purple infernos all over the place. I summoned some of Malachite's beams and shot them at Signus, but he shattered them all with his staff.

"You stand no chance!" he boomed, and drew his staff. He pointed it at us, and a purple laser ripped out and caught Selena's arm. She moved, but the laser had done its work. Her arm was turning into shadow.

I whispered a healing spell, and her arm turned back to normal. I blasted Signus with elemental energy, but he also blocked those.

"We need more projectiles!" I yelled to Selena. She got distracted for a moment, so Signus blasted her with a shadow bolt.

"NO!" I screamed, and dove for her. I summoned a shield of elemental energy around us, and after a few tries of breaking through, he turned to face Sarah and Zach. I hoped that they could keep Signus busy for a bit.

"Selena," I murmured. "You'll be okay, right?" She groaned, and I hoped that meant yes. Her back was almost completely dissolved, so I put my hands on her shoulderslike she had done to me.

I chanted the healing spell, over and over again.

"Come on, Selena. Don't…" I said. I said the healing spell, one last one time, putting all my will and power into the words.

Her eyes closed for a second, and my heart stopped.

"No, Selena…" I gasped. Then her eyes fluttered open.

"Selena!" I exclaimed, and I hugged her. "Are you okay?"

"Not fully healed," she answered. "But better." She felt her back. "Ow

"Thank goodness," I muttered. I helped her up. "Are you okay?" She nodded, and I broke the shield.

Sarah was engaged in combat with Signus. She was totally on fire, and she continued blasting Signus with fireballs.

"Sneak," I whispered to Selena. We slowly walked forward, and Signus didn't pay any attention to us. He seemed totally unharmed, but we were going to change that.

I closed my eyes in concentration.

Then, I sent out a pure white beam of heat at Signus. He screamed in pain and turned around.

"How dare… you…" he gritted his teeth, and slammed his staff against the tiled ground. Signus slammed the staff so hard that he cracked the ground.

Five necromancers rose from the ground.

You'll never get to me!" he cackled, and the necromancers created a shield that he jumped in.

"Get the necromancers. They'll hold the shield, but if we get rid of them, the shield will break." Selena told me.

"Okay." We charged.

The necromancers blasted beams of shadow at us, and we dodged all of them. One of the necromancers whispered something, and a blue green orb flew out. It seemed to be harmless, but it started firing beams at us.

I found the same spell and cast it at the necromancers. They were not as nimble as we were, and one of them got fried to death.

"One down," I muttered. "Four to go." The rest of the casters shot spells at us, and we easily evaded them. Selena dove for the spell tome on the floor, and she grabbed it before any of the skeletons could take it.

I created an elemental shield that blocked the necromancers for just enough time for Selena to escape.

"Even if you defeat Signus," a skeleton whispered. "Abaddon and Betsy are heading straight toward Fort Azari. You don't stand a chance against him."

"And you don't stand a chance against me," I grumbled, and I whispered a spell. I fired a bolt of lightning and zapped the necromancer to ashes.

"Oops…" I grinned, and turned to face the rest of the three necromancers.

They blasted more shadow bolts at me, and this time I wasn't as lucky. One caught me in the chest, and I went flying and I toppled into Abaddon's throne. My chest throbbed with pain.

"Will!" Selena cried. She turned and blasted two necromancers.

Then she turned to face the last one.

"Don't break his shield yet!" she demanded. "You fight for us, okay?" The skeleton nodded and gulped. Selena turned and ran to me.

"Are you okay?" she asked me. Then she saw the hole in my chest. She held out her spell tome and whispered the healing spell.

"Don't you need to open to the right page?" I gulped.

"You just need the spell tome. I memorized the healing spell."

"Not an Airhead anymore," I muttered.

"Hey!"

"Kidding," I laughed. I got up and turned to the necromancer.

"Squeeze the shield until it pops," I commanded. He nodded and moved his hands.

"Ready?" I asked Selena.

"Maybe…" She grabbed my hand for a second, and I felt a burst of strength in my body.

"Let's go." The bubble exploded, and Signus hopped out, fully healed.

"Betrayer!" he snarled. The necromancer gulped.

"Fire as many things as you can!" I yelled. "Signus can't handle too many projectiles!"

"We'll see about that." he growled, and we launched into battle once again, one on one this time, me against Signus.

...

I was so glad that the necromancer had thought to give Zach, Sarah, and Randy a spell tome each. Otherwise, we would have been dead. I drew Malachite and summoned a bucket load sword projectiles to aid me in my fight.

Signus evaded and dodged all my attacks. He slashed with the staff and occasionally fired blasts of shadow at me. Then, the spells started firing.

A few of the turquoise orbs I saw floated out, and blasted Signus. My spirits floated out and tried to latch onto him. Blasts of shadow magic flared out from the necromancer. The Eternal Flame above my head blasted him, and soon he was overwhelmed. (I also saw a tin can hit him, but I'm not sure where it came from.)

"No..." Signus yelped, and he leaped out the window.

"I have to follow him," I said.

"NO!" Randy yelled.

"I'll go too!" Selena volunteered. "I can fly."

"DON'T!" Sarah yelled. "You'll-"

"Watch us," I said to them, and we leaped out the window.

...

We saw Signus, flying up high, circling the island, trailing some sort of dust behind him.

"He's trapping us with a border!" Selena gasped. "Even if we defeat him, we still might be trapped."

"But let's get Signus out of the way first," I said, gliding next to Selena.

"Coward!" I shouted. "Stand and fight!" Signus stopped sprinkling his borders, and he left a gap in the border.

Although there was a hole, the dust crept closer, slow but steady. Signus growled. "You fools!"

"Are you just a big chicken?" Selena yelled next to me. I drew Malachite. Behind us, Sarah, Zach, Randy, and the necromancer fired spells at Signus.

"Let's go," I said to Selena. I flew forward and turned up behind him.

Below, the armies of shadow monsters watched.

Selena charged him in the front, and I came up behind him. I bolted forward and almost struck him when he flinched and lashed out with his staff.

We battled against him, but he fought with centuries more experience than us.

Just as I got ready to strike him again, he yelled, and a shower of darkness hailed from the sky.

"NO!" I screamed, and we dived for cover while Signus cast shadow balls at us. The shower ended, and the ground was littered with darkness infernos.

"You will never stop us!" Signus screamed, and he blasted dark magic at us. We easily evaded them, but Signus was getting tired of playing with us.

"We have to stop him quick," I shouted to Selena. "He's still playing with us. Use all your might!"

"Okay. Sarah?" Selena agreed. Sarah burst into flames and sprouted wings. She flew toward us.

"Zach, can you fly in any sort?" Selena yelled.

"No. I'll stay here and cast spells."

"Okay." We turned to face Signus.

"THIS ENDS NOW!" Signus screamed. He burst into dark flames.

"My pleasure," I shouted back. And then, we made our final charge at Signus.

...

Signus was going crazy now, and we were lucky to have Sarah there with us.

He cast balls of shadow and fired shadow rays at us. He raised his staff and called in some of his own spirits.

"Go spirits!" I yelled, and they engaged in battle with the shades. I summoned a few projectiles and sent them toward Signus. Selena summoned a tornado and flew toward Signus. She shot lightning from her tornado.

"Whoa," I gasped. "She can do that?"

"Yeah, I guess so," Sarah said. She charged Signus, her hands crackling with energy.

"Let's go," I said to myself.

We slashed and hacked at Signus, but he seemed to be growing darker at the minute.

"He's trying to reveal his true form!" Selena yelled. "When he does that, look away!" The battle seemed like a draw. We sometimes got close to him and damaged him a bit, but he was also wearing us down.

My spirits were gone now, although Zach, from the castle, was summoning more. Signus slashed at me with his staff, and a deep burn appeared on my arm.

"AHH!" I flew away for a bit, and I whispered the healing spell. My arm immediately healed.

"Don't get close to the ground!" Selena warned. I looked down. The shadow ghouls were blowing flames up into the air. They weren't reaching us, but they still forced us to get higher.

Signus went into some kind of trance. His whole body was enveloped in purple flames. He started floating toward the sky.

"LOOK AWAY NOW!" Selena screamed. We turned, and I saw a blinding flash of light, and a huge explosion.

I got thrown away, but I willed myself to turn around. Signus looked as good as ever, and he was smiling evilly. I wondered why he was grinning, because he was now getting overwhelmed.

Then I saw what he was looking at.

Selena hadn't been as lucky with the explosion. She was blown against the mountain, and I flew back to the throne room.

"Zach, you go out to fight. I need to get Selena." I touched his hand for a bit, trying to transfer my energy into his body. He suddenly seemed rejuvenated, and he flew out the window.

Selena didn't look good. She had a red rash on her forehead, and her arm was bent at an unnatural angle.

I took out my spell tome and chanted the healing spell over and over again. It didn't help.

"It's not working!" I hollered up to Randy. For a few seconds, there was no answer, but finally, he yelled, "You might be too tired to work with the spells now."

"No," I said quietly. I held her in my arms. "Selena. Come back to me. Please." She didn't move. "SELENA!" I put all my will into the words. "SELENA, PLEASE DON'T..." My words echoed through the island, and down to the city.

"SELENA!" All the lights flickered out. All the energy was transferred to my body. I put my hand on her forehead. When I removed it, all the blood was gone. The gash was healed. I heard very shallow breathing, and my heart leaped. She was alive, for now.

I jumped up, completely healed of any past wounds, and I jumped, for the last time against Signus, into battle.

Signus didn't even stand a chance. I saw Sarah and Zach getting battered down.

He turned and looked at me.

"Sad that your friend died?" he mocked. "Oh well." My hands sparked, and I unleashed another round of electricity, this one even more powerful than the one from earlier.

"AHH!" Signus screamed, and he was pushed back into the ground. There was a huge explosion, and a few shadow ghouls disintegrated.

I thought that he was a goner for good, but he came out of the hole.

"You... you..." Signus trembled with anger. He sent tendrils of shadows at us, and he pulled us close to him. He opened his hand, and a tiny shadow flame danced in his hand.

"Which one of you should I kill first?" he said, "You! The boy comes close…" Sarah and Zach looked at me for help. I forced a confident smile. I closed my eyes in concentration, and tried to ignore the ringing pain on my hand. Soon, my whole body was on fire, and I was trying not to scream in pain.

Then it happened.

A ripple of energy blasted forth from me. Even the flames that were on my body dispersed. I shot off sparks of energy and light. The ripple sent a tremor in the ground, and I heard a cracking sound.

The whole island was breaking apart.

"I'm on your side, kid," Signus said. "That was amazing. You just broke Reality. Almost never see that. You're smart, annoying, and your friend down there is smart too. But don't say that I still don't hate you!"

"Go to Fort Azari and protect it," I told him.

"Well, you're not the boss of me, boy. I'm going there anyway."

"Can you bring anyone else with you?" I asked.

"Yeah. I'll get the flaming girl, the protector, and the guy I spent so hard getting. See you there!"

"What? Wait! Can you remove the border?" But he was already gone. The island shook again.

"I have to get Selena," I muttered to myself.

Luckily, she was conscious and could sort of walk. I flew to her.

"You know how in the vision, Aer said to trust yourself?" I asked her.

"Yeah…"

"I think that you should use that skill now." We flew to the top of the tower in Abaddon's castle. I watched the armies running away in terror from the island. I heard more cracks, and I looked down. The whole caste was breaking apart. Suddenly, I remembered the whole point of going here in the first place.

"The Key of Nightmares!" I gasped. "Do you have that?"

"I left it in the castle!"

"Wait here," I told her. "I'll get it." I jumped down a crack in the building. Rocks were falling from the ceiling. I saw the Key of Nightmares on the ground.

"There!" I said to myself. I scrambled towards it, but suddenly, the whole castle lurched, and the key flew out the window.

"NO!" I yelled, and I flew back out. "The key fell out a window! Let's go!"

"Ready?" she yelled, and the whole tower collapsed. We grabbed each other and jumped.

The wind roared in my ears, and I saw Selena direct the keys to herself. She grabbed the key, and we flew into a steep glide.

"The border!" I yelled, and we turned toward the border, which was almost closed completely.

"Let's go!" Selena screamed, and we sped toward the tiny exit. I held onto her for dear life, and we flew out. The shapes and even time seemed to bend.

I heard an explosion that I later figured out was a sonic boom. I looked behind, and I saw Abaddon's island crumbling to pieces. I saw his throne falling down onto the rough gray ground and splitting into a thousand pieces. It was a great sight to see that we had accomplished our mission, but little did we know that there was much more to come.

Chapter 9

What we saw was not good. The Corruption had almost spread to the borders, and what the Weather Channel said correct (for once).

There was a solar eclipse happening, and it was supposed to last until about three in the morning.

We glided over the walls and landed down next to Allen. Selena's face turned red.

"We have to get Abaddon over here now," he said. "He's too distracted, and it's already eleven thirty." Selena took the Key of Nightmares and raised it to the sky.

Suddenly, an elemental surge of energy dissolved the key. I heard a roar from very far away. Then, in the distance, a huge dragon appeared. Riding it was a very scary man. His face was shrouded in shadows, but I could see his purple, piercing eyes. He had two large horns on his head. He had dark armor on, and he carried two swords that were shooting purple sparks. I knew who he was. He was Abaddon, the Lord of Night. Behind him, a huge army of even more shadow ghouls, necromancers, and a new monster that I didn't know marched.

I heard him cackling even from a distance. "They don't know what they're up against..."

Suddenly, there was a huge explosion of pale gray and blue dust. Alluvion appeared.

"I've come," he said. "Good job taking on Signus." I smiled at him.

"Will," Selena said to me. "Those down there are night warriors. One hit from their spears, and you're pretty much dead, so avoid those for me, okay?"

"Okay."

"Don't die." She grinned.

"Cheers." And the battle has begun.

We went up to the wall. I saw Yohan, Connor, Allen, Zach, and Sarah already up there. Alluvion and Signus were on the central tower, surveying the area.

We first got the advantage, because Alluvion fogged up the whole area and rained down spikes onto the enemy.

I saw that Betsy had eight vines now, which we all had to rip off before we could actually really damage her. The Eternal Flame above my head crackled and shot bolts of energy at the monsters.

When the fog cleared, most of the ghouls were gone, but all the dark warriors and necromancers were still there.

Most of Fort Azari's inhabitants were grouped in sections of gods on towers that lined the walls. They were doing a good job of destroying the enemies. Soon, all the shadow ghouls were gone, and a few necromancers and dark warriors were killed.

Then, Abaddon attacked. The necromancers blasted beams of death at the people. The dark knights raised their spears to the sky, and a beam of dark energy formed. It was sent to Aphelion's tower, and a good chunk of the tower fell out.

"Why did Abaddon let the shadow ghouls die?" I wondered out loud.

"Maybe-" Selena responded, but we saw the cause.

The shadows left behind formed into a giant skull.

"Another dragon?" I groaned. The shadows formed two wings and four feet. Then, a massive tail appeared, and the monster was fully formed.

"Most dragons have a weak spot," Selena murmured. "It's usually a different color..." The dragon was mostly purple and black, but its tail seemed to be made out of various crystals.

"Well, the tail... Airhead," I said to Selena. "Duh."   "I knew that," Selena snorted, and then yelled. "TARGET THE TAIL!"

"Should we go out and fight?" I asked Selena.

"Sure. Let's go."

We flew out into the battlefield and jumped onto the dragon's back. It reared and took off in flight. Projectiles flew after us from the necromancers, but the dragon took most of the impact. As expected, when one blast of shadows hit the tail, it reared in pain.

"How do you stay on this thing!" Selena screamed.

"You don't!" I yelled, and my head formulated the stupidest, most risky pain ever.

I let go of the dragon.

"WILL!" Selena screamed. "NO!" But I caught the dragon's tail, pulling it down towards the ground.

"Dragon!" I screamed. "You're mine now! What do you want to be called?" The dragon roared, and I heard it say in my mind: *Darkecho. Darkecho.*

"Okay. Darkecho."

"What?" Selena yelled.

"He wants to be called Darkecho," I said. "Okay, Darkecho. Could you give us a ride?" The dragon nodded and flapped its wings.

"Are you a he?" I yelled. *Yes*, his voice said in my mind *Brownies.*

"Okay then. But why aren't you fighting for the bad guys?"

Because I don't want to. They don't give me brownies.

"Okay." I said. "Let's go." We sat on him, and he flew up into the air.

"Who should we attack first?" Selena wondered. But Darkecho was already doing his own thing. He dove into the shadow warriors, tossing them aside. One of them through his spear at me, and we ducked. It just grazed my shoulder, but my arm exploded in pain.

Selena noticed me and she groaned. "I told you not to get hit by them." I managed a smile, but the pain was unbearable.

"Darkecho, fly us back to base," Selena commanded. He didn't listen. He kept on plowing through enemies, while in my mind, he asked, *Should I listen to her too Brownies?*

"Yeah," I managed. "Also listen to her… please…"

Afterward, I only saw splotches of what happened. Selena comforting me. The dragon flying back to Fort Azari. Then, when Selena spoke the healing spell, I felt better.

"I can get up-"

"No, Will. Rest a bit." Selena held me down. After about ten minutes, I felt a lot better, and I got up.

I surveyed what had happened during my time down. Aphelion's tower was completely destroyed, and the people who were on it had moved down to the central tower and were casting flames at the enemy.

My Eternal Flame was gone and was now floating in the middle of the central tower, giving Aphelion's children strength. Allen's cabin, the Grovites, was on the front battle lines, growing vines to trip the enemy. Some other people were down there, battling against the hordes of monsters. The rest of the walls looked fine, so I thought we were doing okay. Then, I saw that the Corruption was super close to the edge of the walls. Alluvion came up to me.

"Could you transfer some energy to me?" he requested. "The Corruption's getting awfully close, and I can hold it back, but I need some elemental energy."

"Sure," I said, and I touched his hand. I got a bit more tired, and Alluvion seemed to straighten up more.

"Thanks," he grinned. "Also, your friend Selena told me to tell you to stay here, so I guess you're not going to follow her?"

"Yeah."

"Great," Alluvion said. "I can get you down."

"Sure." A cloud of mist appeared beneath my feet, and I hovered down. I saw Selena and Zach, actually battling Abaddon. Darkecho was fighting against Betsy, and it seemed like a draw. The solar eclipse was helping Darkecho, but the vines on Betsy's wings were harder to get at Darkecho's tail. I was pretty sure that my new dragon friend would be fine, so I flew toward Abaddon.

I wondered where Signus was, and I saw him battling against Betsy too, which was probably a good choice.

Selena and Zach were getting pretty overwhelmed with all of Abaddon's deadly attacks. I floated quickly and landed on top of him before he could do anymore harm.

"AHH!" Abaddon yelled, and he tried to swat me off.

"Will!" Zach exclaimed, and he grinned. Abaddon's head burst into flames, so I had to jump off.

From close up, Abaddon was even more terrifying. He was at least eight feet tall, and now, his blades were flaming.

"I've been expecting you," he said, a grin on his mouth. "More people to kill! I love it!"

"You won't kill me!" I growled.

"Oh!" Abaddon grinned. "He's getting mad, real mad." Then, my temper exploded. I unleash a ripple of elemental energy. I even cleansed the Corruption in a wide area around me. All the monsters lost their balance and fell down around me. Even Abaddon stumbled for a second.

That gave us a chance to attack. The Grovites pushed the warriors back a few yards, and we seemed to be doing good.

Then, everything went wrong.

"Stand your ground!" Abaddon yelled while he was fending us off. The army listened immediately, and they stopped. The dark warriors spears jutted out, and two Grovites were hit. They fell to the ground, and some other people tried to heal them, but I knew that it was no use. Their bodies went slack, and I closed my eyes. The first casualties in a war.

I opened my eyes again and knew that I had to fight for them. I wouldn't want their deaths to be wasted on nothing. We had to win this battle.

I turned to Abaddon.

"You caused their deaths," I snarled. "You will pay for this." I attacked like a cat. I was super nimble, but still attacked ferociously. Even Abaddon was surprised, but got over it in a moment. He laughed. "Mad now aren't you?" He drew his swords and slashed and swiped at me. Although we were using our all, Abaddon was still just playing with us.

Suddenly, with a quick swipe of his blades, he brought his sword up to my throat. I took a risky idea, but because I was about to die, I guess it was okay. I threw Malachite, and it elongated into a sword and smacked into Abaddon's chest plate. He looked down, aghast at the gash in his armor and the knife stuck in it.

"Keep him in the light!" I yelled. He'll heal if he's in shadows!"

"Okay!" someone said, from the main tower, but Abaddon was too fast. The Eternal Flame shined onto Abaddon just after he ripped Malachite out of his chest and threw it onto the ground.

"I will never be stopped!" Abaddon growled.

"Retreat!" Randy's voice called.

"We'll finish this off in your precious fort." Abaddon said, and he flew away.

We got back behind the walls of the fort, and I saw Alluvion.

"Alluvion!" I yelled, and he walked over. "How much Corruption did you repel?"

"I pushed it back ten meters or so. I could've pushed back more, but I didn't want to use all my strength."

"How much more time did you give us?" I asked.

"An hour or so, the magical barrier is about to break. I need to go help that." He walked off.

A few minutes later, I heard a huge explosion. The main gate rattled as the monsters pounded on it. I found Selena with Zach.

"Ready, Mumbo Jumbo?" Selena asked me.

"That's my new nickname, Airhead?" I grinned.

"Yep."

"Oh well…" The gates rattled and shuddered. "Here we go." The iron bars cracked and snapped in two, and the dark knights funneled through. All of us blasted them at the same time, and as the powers combined, it became elemental energy that crackled and exploded on the first row of knights.

But the power didn't stop there.

The energy kept on building from all of us, until it could hold no longer. The elemental energy balled up and suddenly shrank. Everything was quiet for a moment.

The ball exploded. Everyone was thrown back. The ball still was there though. It released surge after surge of energy, and after firing a bit, it released turquoise balls of sinning energy.

"Reality?" Selena murmured. The air crackled, and in a huge blue-green explosion, a man appeared.

He wore flowing turquoise robes and had a white shirt and pants underneath it. He had a timeless face that looked perfect, without a spot, and he held, strangely, a piece of fabric.

"Oh no," Abaddon muttered. "Reality just has to ruin things!" Reality tore the cloth at the seams and disappeared with the orb. There was an awkward silence for a few seconds.

"Bah!" Abaddon said. "False alarm. Charge ahead!" Suddenly, the orb appeared again, this time even brighter. It blasted elemental energy at the few knights who were still fighting.

Then, the ground started shaking, and the main tower started cracking.

"Maybe not a good thing!" Selena yelped, and she dove for cover. The dark storm clouds above turned blue-green, and my heart turned cold.

"Not storm weavers again!" Zach wailed. Luckily, it wasn't. A storm of turquoise orbs hailed from the sky. They drilled into the knight's armor and broke the necromancers attempt to create a shield.

Although the rain was really effective, they also destroyed a lot of the walls. Once the rain stopped, Abaddon's forces gathered together again, but were shredded by the orb that still guarded the entrance.

"Charge!" Abaddon yelled, and they went around the orb.

Alluvion snapped his fingers, and the building smashed down on top of them. Abaddon was in the wreckage, but he easily dug himself out.

"You will never stop me!" he screamed, but Reality's "tearing at the seams" was not over. Another earthquake started, and Abaddon fell on his face. The monsters rushed forward and attacked, and while we were distracted, Abaddon rushed in front of all of us.

"After him!" I yelled, and Selena and Allen flew after him. Allen grew vines and tried to get his attention.

"Gotta get the Eternal Flame!" I yelled, and rushed back. It was still hanging in the air.

"Darkecho!" I called. The purple dragon swooped in, and I gave him instructions on what to do.

Your favorite dragon at your service! He said in my mind.

"Thanks," I laughed. I grabbed the Eternal Flame and willed it to float out toward Abaddon.

The dragon flew me straight to Abaddon, and once again I jumped on top of him.

"AAGHH!" Abaddon screamed. "STOP DOING THAT! I WAS JUST ABOUT TO KILL THIS NAUGHTY GIRL HERE!" He brushed me off his head before I could stab him. I looked deep into Abaddon's eyes. His piercing glare drilled through me, but I could see a little fear in his eyes, even a little respect for us.

Suddenly, his glare almost did drill through me, because his eyes shot a dark laser. Selena pushed me down, and I watched as the laser drilled through the dirt.

"Thanks." I said, getting back up.

"Do you wanna fight?" Allen demanded at Abaddon. "Or are you just going to stand there?" Instead of answering, Abaddon's gloved, black hands burst into purple flames.

"Fight," We charged him, but he just disappeared and reappeared behind us. I willed the Eternal Flame to grow even brighter, and Abaddon stopped teleporting.

"I'm still just playing with you," he snarled. I launched a blue projectile at him, but he crossed his two swords and the beam shattered.

"Projectiles," Selena suggested. "The same thing with Abaddon, if we fire enough projectiles at him all at once, he'll be overwhelmed.

"Okay," Allen said. He forced the roots to grow even higher. They were alive, snapping at Abaddon's feet. Allen cast green sparkles at Abaddon.

"Homing projectiles," Selena added.

"Homing?" I asked.

"Oh! You know. Malachite's sword beams. They track your enemy down."

"Okay." Selena summoned herself a wind tornado and flew toward Abaddon, the energy from her storm crackling. A white beam of energy lashed out, but Abaddon was already busy with everything else. He was blasted back, but he went out of the light, so his wounds closed immediately.

Selena raised her wind blade, and a bolt of lightning flew from the sky and ricocheted off the blade and flew into Abaddon.

"I - I am invincible in the darkness!" he yelled.

"But not in the light," I muttered, and I advanced, summoning more projectiles along the way.

"No!" he screamed. And he flew away.

"Don't let him get away!" I screamed, and we flew up into the air.

"You'll never catch me!" Abaddon yelled, but the Eternal Flame shot a bolt of heat and hit him. He blocked the bolt with his swords, but he was tiring because he was in the light.

"We can't stop him with the solar eclipse," Selena said. "We can work together and summon the sun again."

"But last time you did that, you almost blew up!"

"I think I'll have more control now."

"Okay. I'm up for crazy ideas." We drifted to the ground and linked hands. I closed my eyes in concentration, and I felt Selena's power flowing into my body. I felt myself grow hotter and hotter.

I heard Abaddon screaming. "LITTLE RUNT!" I forced myself to open my eyes, and I saw Selena, glowing white. I turned and saw Allen, pushing Abaddon back into the Meeting House.

I lost concentration and we unleashed a glowing aura of power all around us. Some of it clashed into Abaddon, and he collapsed. We ran up to him, and I demanded, "Are you on our side now?"

"I'm sorry…" Abaddon groaned. "Just please don't kill me…"

"Force him onto our side!" Selena said. "He's trying to trick you!"

"What?" I said. I felt bad for him, and I knelt down close to him.

"A little parting gift…" he murmured. Suddenly, he lashed out with his swords and pinned me down to the ground.

"I'm sorry," he grinned. "I'll have to kill you anyway. Yharon wanted you alive, but it's just too hard."

"Will!" Selena shouted. Abaddon shot a blast of shadow magic behind him, and I guess that shut Selena up.

"Here we go. I'm sorry." He brought his sword up, and jabbed downwards. Suddenly, a spike flew out and shattered his sword.

"WHAT!" he screamed, and he turned. "Alluvion. You know that you stand no chance against me." He fired a shadow laser from his hand and smashed him into the Meeting House. I dashed toward him, looking for an opening. Allen ran forward too and summoned more vines to trip Abaddon.

"He drew his remaining sword. I thought that he was going to fight with it, but instead, he threw it and the nearest target, who was Allen. He crumpled to the ground.

"NO!" Selena screamed.

"I surrender," Abaddon admitted. "You guys pick a good fight, but I had to kill someone, right?"

"YOU'VE GONE TOO FAR!" Selena screamed. She was so ferocious that she even scared me.

Abaddon probably was trying to trick us again, because he summoned shades all around him. I ran forward too, but I sort of was too late, because

Selena already had killed all the shades and had her sword pointed at Abaddon's throat.

"Don't destroy him," I pleaded (I sort of forgot that he was a god and that we couldn't destroy him). "Just... bind him." We linked hands again and summoned rainbow chains and left Abaddon sitting there. Selena's part of the chains was molten red, her anger, and my side was pure white.

I saw that the rest of Fort Azari had defeated the necromancers and the dark knights. Selena and I rushed up to Allen, and she cradled him in her lap, crying.

I knew that no amount of healing could save Allen. The shadows had already gotten to his soul. I crouched down near Selena and sat down.

"Should I pull the sword out?" I suggested. Selena just nodded.

"Help me," I said, and we drew the sword out. I spoke the healing spell and tried to mend the shadows.

"I can't believe... Abaddon," Selena sniffled. I hugged her and tried to comfort her.

"When you ran away," I said. "Was he with you?"

"Yes," she answered

"Tell me about it."

"Okay... When I came out, Allen found me. He was also wandering the streets. We became best friends... he... he helped me so much. We once got lost in a nymph's cave. He saved my life so many times." She smiled, thinking of the thoughts. "He was a hero, Will. A true hero."

"Where do the souls go?" I asked her.

"To Aphelion… They get judged for their deeds. And then they either go to paradise forever, do nothing forever, or get tortured forever." She buried her head in my shoulder.

"I'm sorry."

"Abaddon…" She gritted her teeth. "I still just can't believe that he would do such a thing… I can't believe…" She started crying again. The demigods gathered in a circle around us. Nina came forward and said to Selena, "I'm so sorry." I blinked out tears. Allen must have been really important if even Nina would be nice to Selena. I also was sad that I didn't get to meet any of the demigods who had perished in the battle.

We sat there, in the middle of the battlefield for the rest of the solar eclipse.

"Are you better?" I asked quietly.

"Um… I hope," she muttered.

"Let's go, Airhead." I said, and we stood up.

Chapter 10

The rest of the night/day was bittersweet. Three Grovites and one Cryonite had died during the battle.

In the afternoon, Selena and I sat on the pier, watching some demigods rowing a canoe.

"You've missed a lot with the quest," she said. "We have the sniper battles on Friday."

"When is that, again?"

"Day after tomorrow, I can't wait for it." I heard footsteps pounding behind us. It was Nina.

"Hey!" she yelled. "Randy wants to see you. It's about Abaddon."

"Ruined our one actually peaceful moment," I muttered. "We'll get back here later. Let's go."

…

We heard the arguing from half a mile away.

"Needs Vesuvius!" I heard Abaddon yell. We walked into the Meeting Room. Randy turned to face us.

"Will and Selena. You're finally here. Abaddon won't withdraw the Corruption completely unless we get the other legendary weapon."

"If you get Vesuvius, I'll have confidence supporting you! Just… I'll stop the Corruption for now, but still… come on!"

"We can go!" I suggested.

"No," Randy answered. "You need a break. We're going to send Zach though…"

"WHAT!" Selena yelled. "Why don't you…"

"Some people are jealous of you. I'm afraid of that. But Yohan and Connor are also going."

"It's okay, Selena. We'll stay here." Selena's face still was red.

"Where'd Sarah go?" I asked, trying to change the subject.

"Oh!" Randy said. "She'll be staying here. She explained to her dad that she was on a summer camp. She won't be staying during the school year though."

"Oh."

"You sound disappointed," Selena snorted.

"Am not!" I grumbled.

"Sure."

"Can we be back up?" I suggested. "In case they get trapped or anything."

"Okay," Randy said.

"Can we leave now?" Selena asked. Randy nodded, and we walked off.

"Until the eighteenth of June!" I heard Abaddon yell.

"Another deadline?" I muttered. "How many do they want?" I turned to face Selena. "Look, Selena. I'm sorry. But we really can't do anything about it. You think we could"

"Leave by ourselves?" Selena's face brightened. "How about after the sniper battles. We could leave…"

"Without permission?" I asked when we reached the pier.

"Yeah." She dangled her legs over the water, and I did the same.

"I like it!" I grinned. "Well, we better prepare!"

"Yeah." The sun slowly dipped down and touched the horizon. "We should eat dinner soon." The boat in the lake suddenly flipped.

"Oops," Yohan laughed from behind us. He sat down on the pier next to us and brushed some of his blond hair out of his eyes. "We're leaving tomorrow morning. It's apparently a big emergency and stuff."

"Well, that's cool," I said. "Good luck. I know you'll do good."

After, dinner, we just came back to the same spot, this time with Zach.

"Where's Yharon's fortress anyway?" I asked.

"In the Amazon jungle." he answered. "We're going to use my tracking senses to find his fortress. You probably could do it too, Will." Selena looked and me and grinned.

"That's cool," I said. "Oh yeah, Zach. Does there happen to be any way to communicate with us other than phones? You know… cause there's probably no signal in the jungle."

"Oh!" Selena exclaimed. "Because the Corruption was coming so close before, you never had spell-casting class. So we pretty much have to memorize all of the spells on a spell tome. The ones we got from the necromancers were more powerful, but it didn't have a communication spell in it."

"Is there any way to boost your energy somehow?" I asked. "Because I couldn't cast any spells because I didn't have any energy."

"Yeah," Zach answered. "You can get energy potions. Some alchemists, usually Grovites, make energy potions. Don't trust them too much, though. Once, someone accidentally put some poison ivy in it, and the person who drank it got a rash for a year."

"Really?"

"Yeah," Selena said. "That person who gave the potion was most definitely not Zach."

"Sorry!" Zach muttered, his face turning red.

"You really did that once?" I laughed.

"Umm… yeah. But it was a mistake! I thought that the poison ivy was a root! And I didn't pay attention to why my hand was red." I laughed. "Good job…"

We sat there for a few minutes, chatting and talking about stuff and all that I missed. It almost felt like I was normal, chatting with my friends, almost.

…

Because I had such a great day that day, I was sure that something would go wrong the next day.

I hoped not, but, of course, it happened.

"We need to dump Will in the lake!" Nina gasped when we were in spells class.

"Oh no," I muttered. "I hate water. I'm not going in."

"All newcomers do!" Nina insisted.

"Please no!" I said.

"Let's do it after dinner!" someone suggested. Selena looked at me. "You'll be fine, okay."

"But I've never been good with water! Does Aquaia have some kind of grudge against Galaxius, or something?" Selena's face darkened.

"Well," she said. "Galaxius doesn't really appreciate Aquaia's underwater palace, no offense. He said that it's too stuffy, and the air conditioning's turned on too high, and… well. You get the idea. So Aquaia's been mad ever since. So it's been really difficult to control water lately for elementals."

"What's lately?"

"Oh! Past five hundred years or so."

"Um…"

"So now, Galaxius is in Aer's palace," Selena said. "Much nicer up there, I think."

"Oh!" I said, suddenly remembering something. "Who's the god of nature? I've been wanting to ask you that."

"No one. It's all around us, nature but as humans begin populating the world, nature fades away. It's so sad."

"Okay, then."

The rest of the day went fine.

I had potions class after that, but I accidentally blew up most of the materials after I saw that I could control most of the various chemicals and plants.

Then, we practiced archery, and I was pretty good at it.

"Our sniper battles use bows and arrows," Selena explained. "We don't use sharp arrows, but there are many different types that we have to make in the forging class. You know the one where you broke the hammer."

"Yeah," I laughed.

"Okay."

"What are the teams?" I asked.

"Well, sometimes we go in pairs of two, sometimes we're cut into two teams, and sometimes there are three groups, and my personal favorite, cabins make their own alliances by convincing people. There could be a wide amount of results of teams, but they all have to stay in their cabin teams. No splitting up."

"What are we doing tomorrow?"

"We're doing groups of two."

"How do you win?"

"Well, for groups of two, you have to capture a team's stone. It's a shiny yellow rock, easy to see. Once you capture their stone, they become out. Randy surveys the whole area and finds out teams who are out. The last ones standing are the winners. Also, if a team takes out a team with many stones, they get all of them. There is some luck involved, but it's mostly skill. There also are monsters in the area we're going to, so beware."

"Where are we going to go?"

"The volcano."

"What types of monsters are there?"

"Many. There are hidden boulder type monsters called Corites. Also, there are monsters like nymphs called Volcanians. And their relatives wield deadly claws. They're called Selenians named after me, Yay."

"What?"

"Yeah."

We headed over to the mountain to make arrows, and this time, I didn't break anything. Another Aphelist called John taught me about all the different types of arrows I could make.

"Who am I teamed up with?" I asked Selena.

"You choose that yourself," she told me.

"Okay."

My last class of the day was a monster class, where we learned about all the horrific breeds of monsters.

Nothing went wrong even there. Although I thought that the class was boring, I wished that it would go on forever, because I now dreaded the water even more than before.

Finally, we finished class and we got some free time. I went out with Selena to the lake.

Although it was crystal clear and I could even see Aquaia's cabin down there, I still was nervous.

Suddenly, I thought I saw a tentacle flailing about in there.

"Are there monsters down there?" I asked Selena nervously.

"Not that I know of," she answered. "The only water monster that actually is a threat is a kraken, and they're so rare. Also, Aquaia's children live down there. We would never put any monsters."

I still wasn't sure.

We had dinner, and Nina asked Randy if they could throw me into the lake. He agreed, and Nina flashed a mischievous smile to me. After we finished dinner, I was going to walk back to my cabin to escape getting thrown into the water.

Before I could do that, I felt someone grab my shoulder. It was a Cryonite. More people gathered behind him, and they carried me and threw me into the lake.

I created a huge splash, and just as I came out of the water, a tentacle lashed out. It grabbed my waist and raised me up into the air.

I reached for Malachite, and drew it, but it didn't do anything against the hard, scaly skin of the monster.

"HELP!" I screamed. I turned, and I saw the monster as it rose in its full glory out of the water.

It had so many green, slimy tentacles flicking out into the air. And to top it all off, it had a huge, blue shell, and I could see one huge, black eye looking straight at me.

"I AM ABYSSION!" he yelled, and his voice echoed across the whole rolling landscape.

"Who are you?" Nina screamed. "We haven't learned about you…"

"THE FORGOTTEN ONE!" he boomed. "NO ONE KNOWS ABOUT ME ANYMORE. I AM FORGOTTEN, SO I SEEK REVENGE ON ANYONE WHO ENTERS MY HOME TERRITORY!"

"Charge!" Nina yelled, and she fired a bolt of frost at Abyssion. He roared, and the icy blast splattered against his shell like nothing. He squirted black ink, and everyone dived for cover.

"HELP!" I screamed again.

"Cover your face!" I heard Randy yell. I put my shirt up on my face, and I could still smell the putrid scent of the toxic acid. When it cleared away, I saw that all the trees had burned away and were smoking.

"What do we" Suddenly, Abyssion blasted my face with water. I knew that I might die pretty soon, so I threw Malachite straight at him. It smacked against his shell, and it cracked. He roared in pain and finally dropped me.

Not in the right place though.

I landed on the dock and smashed my head pretty hard. After that, my vision was pretty blurry. I saw Selena rush up to me. She dragged me away behind a bush, and I saw some Aphelists blasting Abyssion with fire. One of them reached down, grabbed Malachite from his shell, and flew back.

"Here," he said, and dropped Malachite at my feet.

"Are you okay, Will?" Selena murmured.

"Yeah," I croaked.

"I should probably get my spell tome, but I'll try to do the spell here." She spoke the words to the healing spell, and I felt a bit better.

"I'll be fine," I said, but right after that, I fell unconscious.

...

I'll have to thank Alluvion for this. I could control myself, thank the gods, and I was right above Abyssion's shell. He was firing blue bolts at the Aphelists, but they dodged most of his attacks.

I guess Abyssion remembered his tentacles, because he suddenly lashed out with two of them. I wanted to cry out, but my voice wouldn't work.

Two of the Aphelists saw the attack coming, but one didn't and he got smashed into the water.

Get me out of this dream! I thought to Alluvion, but the only answer I got was, *I'm coming!*

He definitely was coming.

There was a huge explosion of mist, and Alluvion appeared.

"Excuse me," he said calmly. "Has Aquaia been monitoring you?"

"Alluvion," Abyssion snarled. "You know you can't defeat me."

"Sure I can't by myself, but we have the full force of Fort Azari here." My dream faded away.

...

"Full force of Fort Azari here." Alluvion's words echoed throughout the grounds.

"Will!" Selena exclaimed. "You're alive! I thought that my healing spell wouldn't work!" She hugged me fiercely, and we got up.

"Let's go murder this guy," I said, and we flew toward Abyssion.

The battle wasn't even close. Alluvion fogged in the whole area, so Abyssion couldn't see, but we still could. Random blasts of water came flying at us, but they all missed. All of us fired attacks at Abyssion, and his shell cracked again.

He roared in pain and screamed, "You've made an enemy, but remember, never enter the water, or you will face my wrath." He exploded in water, and everything became silent.

"The Aphelist who fell!" I yelled. "We have to save him!"

"What?" someone said.

"I was having a dream, and I saw him fall into the water! Randy, you have to save him!"

"But Abyssion said-" Randy held up his hand, and everyone became quiet.

"Will is correct," he said. "Abyssion won't harm any of Aquaia's children." I saw him dive into the water. He came up with a body. I looked into his face, and I saw that he was John, the person I met earlier.

"Can we save him?" I asked. Randy shook his head.

"Please…" I choked on my words. "Just try…"

"It's no use," he said, but I stepped forward anyway. Selena and another boy came up with spell tomes.

"We can't have any more deaths," I murmured, and then I thought in my head. *Reality, sir.*

Hmm?

"Reality!" I said out loud. "Help us!" Two red beams shot from the spell tomes.

"REALITY!" I screamed. "PLEASE!" Suddenly, there was a huge explosion of light, and Reality appeared, holding his cloth.

"He is not dead yet," he murmured. "I will be able to save him. I am doing you a great deed, demigods. You interrupted my evening spa treatment." He summoned a red book from the air, and he started chanting words. A blast of red light burst forth from the book. The light filled the whole air. People who got hurt seemed rejuvenated. The whole air burned. The trees healed.

John started breathing long, rasping breaths.

The whole air shimmered with a red glow. It became brighter and brighter. The night darkness was overwhelmed, and it seemed to be day.

The red glow faded with Reality, and I looked at John. He looked completely fine, and his breathing was smooth. I looked around at everyone. They were shining and seemed a bit taller, stronger, and more perfect. Nina's eyes were more piercing, and she seemed even more terrifying than before.

Randy glowed an iridescent blue. Selena was...
wow. I looked down at myself. I was glowing a
million different colors. Everyone seemed to be
shining.

Suddenly, the sky exploded in color, and it
fell upon us.

"Reality's blessing," Selena murmured.
"Wow." Time seemed to have gone backward. The
sun was still setting, although it had gone down
hours before.

"We should go to sleep," Randy proposed.
"We'll have the sniper battles tomorrow." Everyone
nodded in agreement, and we went back to our
cabins. I was really tired because I hadn't slept in
two days.

I hoped that I would get a good sleep, but of
course, I had a dream.

...

I was in the Amazon jungle. Zach, Yohan,
and Connor were tramping through the deep foliage.

"Up ahead," Yohan said. "There's the
beginning of Yharon's territory. They walked
through the stone walkway.

"Boats?" Connor said. "I guess we could
take them." I wanted to scream: don't do it!

They almost did.

"I'm an Aphelist, though," Yohan pointed
out. "Better not to take it." *Thank you Yohan*, I

thought in my head. They walked up the river on the shore, and up ahead, there was a building that had a banner that said: Welcome tourists, to Yharon's jungle! Please take a brochure for further information.

"What?" Connor laughed. "Tourists come here?" Suddenly, Zach gasped. He appeared to be in some kind of trance.

"It's… it's…" he murmured, and started walking forward.

"Zach?" Yohan yelped. "What- what are you doing?" Zach came up to a tree and started to climb it.

"Zach!" Connor yelled. "No!" The tree started to grow around him. Connor and Yohn tried to pull him out of the tree, but he was glued.

"We'll leave him for now," Yohan suggested. "It's too hard to pull him out." My dream suddenly shattered as the tree moved to encase them too in a tangle of leaves and foilage.

…

I woke up with a start, dressed quickly, and rushed outside to the Meeting House.

Randy was inside with Selena, and I hurried to them.

"Randy!" I yelled. "I had a dream-"

"I know," he said. "Selena had one too." I looked at her, astonished.

"You had-"

"Yeah."

"Well, then, what are we waiting for?" I yelled. "Let's go! C'mon! Zach's in trouble! They're all in trouble! Let's-" Randy held up his hand.

"Someone else should go," he proposed. "Someone who's good at battling against fire." He stepped aside, and out of a room, Nina came out.

"Me," she said.

…

A few hours later, we were on a plane headed straight toward some remote town.

"Tomorrow would be the sixteenth," Selena said. "We'll get there by then."

"That's two days from the deadline," I said.

"Yeah. We'll have time. I wish I could sleep, but I just did," Selena said.

"We are in Aer's territory, right?" I asked her.

"Yeah."

"So maybe, somehow, we could burn some time by going into another dream, and maybe we'll see your mom."

"Craziest idea ever! Let's do it." I closed my eyes and felt Selena lean against me.

We both appeared in a dream, and we saw Aer's palace ahead.

Chapter 11

We floated towards Aer's palace. I tried talking and it worked. We could also move by our own will.

"What are we doing here?" Selena whispered.

"I don't know." The wind brought us down onto Aer's garden, where she was sitting. Now, when I saw her, I was stunned. She definitely resembled Selena, but she just looked more regal and proud. Her dress was made out of white silk that flowed like the wind, and her eyes looked just like a clear blue sky.

"Selena," Aer said. "I am very glad that you came here. Yharon is growing impatient, but he won't be happy to hear that his key got destroyed."

"Mom," Selena said.

"Dear. You have done well. You have made me proud." Aer smiled, and I couldn't help but smile as well.

"But I come to say two things. One, your friend, Zach. He"

"What happened to him?" I shouted out, and then became red. "Sorry, lord."

"Demigods rarely show respect to goddess," Aer said. "I do not care. But, when he got trapped in the tree, do you know what happened?"

"Well, no."

"The tree connected its spirit to him. This happens very rarely, but when it happens, you have to hurry and get him out, otherwise, he'll become part of the tree."

"How much time do we have to save him?" Selena asked.

"Two days and Selena. You will need to trust yourself again. I wish you good luck, and I give both of you my blessing." She opened up her hand, and a wisp of white smoke flew from her hand into our mouths. I think that Selena got a whole lot more. "When you wake up, you'll be arriving."

"Thank you, lord," I said.

"Bye mom!" Selena called, and when she looked away, there were tears in her eyes. Aer waved her hand, and the dream disappeared. It wasn't over, though.

...

We were at New York City. Pieces of Abaddon's island were scattered all over the skyscrapers and the buildings. Purple flames were leaping everywhere, and there was a huge chunk of the Empire State Building missing. Many police cars, ambulances, and T.V. reporters were scattered around the area.

"-think that it might be a meteor that smashed down, but the rock is different than any other we've seen," one reporter said.

"What did we do?" Selena whispered. "I thought that Abaddon's island would just dissolve."

"Oh no," I murmured. "But your dad..."

"I think he's far away enough to not get hit by the "meteor", but I still hope he's okay." Suddenly, there was a rumble, and another part of the Empire State Building fell out and crashed onto the pavement. The dream shattered.

...

We both jolted awake this time. Selena's hand flew out and smashed my face.

"Ow!" I yelped.

"Sorry," Selena grunted. "We're landing. Where'd Nina go, in the first place?"

"No idea..." I answered. "What's this place called anyway?" Suddenly, our seats opened up, and we fell into the open air.

"What?" Selena screamed. We summoned the air, and floated upwards.

Below us was a small encampment. There was a wooden wall bordering the area in a rectangle, and tall towers lined the area. A central courtyard that had a large fire pit in the middle sat in the center of the base, and logs used as chairs were placed around it. Several log cabins like the one used for the Grovites at Fort Azari were plopped around the campfire. I saw people wearing wooden armor and holding green banners running around the area.

Suddenly, a flash of green light flew from a tower and struck Selena in the chest. She went flying back and started drifting slowly toward the ground. I guess she fell like a feather because she was a daughter of Aer.

"Selena!" I screamed, and started flying after her. The wound in her chest started sprouting leaves. Vines creeped around her body, and as I grabbed her, the leaves creeped around my hands too.

I dodged the blasts that came flying at me, but the plants kept crawling around me. I thought that they were just going to annoy me, but they started squeezing just as I touched the ground.

Two people rushed at us, a boy and a girl, and I asked, "Who are you?" Green spots danced around my face, and I was sure that I would lose consciousness soon.

"We are Grovites," the boy said. I noticed that they were all teenagers, like everyone at Fort Azari (except for Randy) were.

"Are you… friends of Fort Azari?" I groaned, falling on the ground.

"Yes. And you?" a girl asked.

"Friend-" But I lost consciousness.

...

I woke up in one of the cabins in a white bed. Selena was next to me because we were still connected with a vine. I reached for my belt and my heart nearly stopped. Malachite wasn't there.

Then, I looked up. There were three more beds next to ours, and there was also a table. I saw my precious knife there, along with Selena's wind blade.

I felt completely fine, but Selena looked pretty bad. Her face was pale, and she was barely breathing.

I looked outside, and it was dark. I was still tired, so I lay back down and fell asleep again. Alluvion was nice to me, and he didn't give me any dreams.

I woke up, feeling really refreshed, until I looked around. I saw a clock hanging the corner. It read June seventeenth. One day. It was six in the morning, apparently.

"Selena," I whispered.

"Uh…" she groaned.

"Good," I laughed. "You're alive."

"What happened," she murmured.

"Well, someone shot some Grovite thing at you, and you got wrapped in vines."

"Uh oh."

"So I grabbed you and flew down. These guys should be on our side. They said that they were friends of Fort Azari."

"Great welcoming gift," Selena muttered. "And, where's Nina?"

"Right here," someone grumbled from another bed.

"She's here," I laughed.

"And why are you in the same bed?" Nina demanded.

"We're stuck together with a vine! That's not our fault!" Selena said.

"Can you get up?" I asked Selena.

"Maybe," she muttered. She stood up and tried to walk. She stumbled and said: "With you, I could…"

"Ok." I could walk easily, so I went to Selena, and she rested her arm on me. We slowly moved outside of the room. I grabbed our weapons while we were going. Sadly, it was overcast outside.

We headed to the central area, and I saw the same boy and girl talking to each other, sitting at the fire. When I looked at them, I saw that the boy looked a bit older than me. He had green hair that appeared to be dyed green, and his eyes were a deep shade of green. A brown chest plate interwoven with green vines was on his chest, and he had leggings the same style, and wore a backpack. *All Grovites*, I thought.

But when the girl turned her head, I got a big scare. She looked so much like Nina. Her eyes were icy blue, and she had a pale face. She seemed to be the same age as the boy, and she wasn't dressed like any of the others. She had on a white coat and had pale blue pants and the hair on her head was startling too. It was blond, but almost white. But even if she looked like Nina, she wasn't as buff or strong as Nina. In my opinion, she looked a lot more graceful and commanding than Nina too.

"Well, they're awake too," she muttered. "Introduce yourself, David."

"You're so annoying," he said. "Well, I'm David, and she's Hannah."

"Where is this place?" I wondered.

"Does Randy tell you anything these days?" Hannah complained. "This is a Grovite encampment. We're supposed to keep watch on Yharon's jungle."

"But you're not a Grovite," Selena noted.

"Of course I'm not a Grovite! Do I look like one? I'm just here from New York, but because someone destroyed Abaddon's island. Half of us were sent here, half of us to Fort Azari."

"Um…" I said, glancing at Selena. "We were the ones who destroyed the island."

"You were?" David's eyes brightened. "Really?"

"Well," Hannah grumbled. "Not what I expected. You just got defeated easily by us."

"But we were taken off guardAnd we need to go!" I said. "Our friends were captured by a tree's spirit, and we only have two days to free them."

"Well, you'll need one of us," David said. "We're pretty much the only ones who can free people from the spirit of a tree."

"Let's go!" Selena urged.

"In your condition?" Hannah laughed. "Not a chance. David is a healer, though. He could..."

"Sure," he said, and took out a staff from his backpack. It was made out of some kind of wood, and there was a green jewel at the end of it. He started chanting words, and a green light burst from the staff. It filled the air, like what Reality had done. The beam was growing brighter now, and suddenly, there was an explosion. The beam died down, and Selena seemed a lot better now. The vine connecting us also dissolved.

"Thanks," I muttered, and then turned to Selena. "You won't need any more support, will you?"

"No, I think I'm fine now." Selena answered.

"So, can we leave now?" I asked again.

"We'll have to ask the head," David said. "So let's go to-" He faltered because there was a loud roar. A blast of fire exploded into the sky.

"Or not," Hannah said. "Yharon's right-hand man is here. I mean right hand woman."

"Solaria." Selena murmured, and the gates on the keep exploded.

…

Abaddon was scary enough. Now, Solaria was a completely different matter.

Now, Solaria was terrifying. Her whole face was blazing with white flames, so I couldn't see her eyes. She had a crown of spiky, red thorns on her head, and the thorns blasted flames everywhere. She had on a white sleeveless dress on, and it burned so bright that her arms and legs just seemed to be flames leaping out of her. She held two balls of fire in her hands.

"WHO DARES COME CLOSE?" she screamed, glaring at everyone.

"We beat her last time," David said. "Barely, But it was raining, so the fires kept on getting put out."

"Will," Selena whispered, and we both flew up into the air.

"Solaria!" I shouted. "I heard how you lost against this place before! Why'd you want to come again? To lose and get embarrassed?"

"Puny human!" Solaria snarled. "An Aerialite. You can't beat me, I'm afraid." She blasted me with a beam of flames, but it just felt warm against my skin. Solaria's smiled faded.

"An elemental?" she said. "I'll take you with me then." She lashed out her arm, and a red-hot hook came flying at me. I drew Malachite and knocked it aside. I fired a spinning blizzard at her, and it smashed against her face.

"YOU... YOU!" And she flew at me.

If it weren't for everything else, I would have been dead in a moment. I first blasted her with elemental energy, and she stumbled.

"YOU DON'T STAND A CHANCE!" Solaria screamed, and she charged at me, firing solar balls of energy. While I attacked her, all the demigods below helped a lot. Green energy and snow were flying up and homing in on Solaria. She knocked them aside with her flames, but she was tiring.

On the other hand, we were also slowing down. The attacks from below slowly waned and turned to nothing. Solaria shot a column of flames at me, and I was knocked to the ground.

"A rain spell?" I yelled desperately. Selena nodded and flew down. Solaria descended down and blasted me with more flames. She summoned some daggers and threw them while she was walking leisurely to me. I rolled aside, but one of them still grazed my hand.

I cried out in pain and fell to the ground. I heard Selena chanting along with some other people. Solaria took another dagger from the air and held it to my neck.

Suddenly, she cried out in pain and dropped the knife. I caught it and threw it at her, but she already was gone. Behind her was Nina, her hands ablaze with blue flames.

"Hello," she said. "Need some help?"

Solaria was still super agile and deadly. She tried to blast Nina, but I was still helping a bit. I managed to fly back up and summoned shields everywhere to annoy Solaria.

Suddenly, she unleashed all her might after she just managed to hit Nina with a blast of fire. She rose into the air, tendrils of fire lashing all around her. She used two of the tendrils and grabbed both of us.

"Strong, eh?" she yelled. "Not too much." A blue light started to fill the area.

"NO!" she screamed, and dropped us onto a building. Nina stayed on, but I took a tumble and almost rolled off the side.

The blue light was growing stronger now. I turned and saw Selena rising into the air, her whole body glowing.

"STOP IT!" Solaria fired a burst of flames at Selena, but they just bounced off her.

The light began to become blinding, so I looked away. Unfortunately, I saw that the cabin we were standing on was on fire. I couldn't avoid the light, so I decided to just watch. Blue beams exploded out from Selena and fizzled out. More of them came streaming out until it felt like I was watching a light show.

There was a rumble of thunder, and the heavens opened up. It began pouring rain, buckets upon buckets. The blue light disappeared, and Selena floated to the ground, her energy drained.

"I- WILL GET- YOU!" Solaria screamed, and she fizzled away, drenched by the water.

For the first time in my time, I enjoyed the rain as it poured down onto the encampment as it put out all the fires burning, including the one in the fireplace. The cabin groaned again, and Selena rushed over.

"Are you okay?" she asked me.

"No," I said. "But get me off the building before it collapses, please!"

"What about Nina?"

"Who cares?" I laughed. Selena picked me up and set me on the ground. She did the same with Nina, but made sure that she went somewhere else. She flew back here and promptly collapsed on the ground next to me.

"You okay?" I muttered.

"Nina's too heavy," Selena groaned.

"Oh well," I laughed, staring into the endless gray clouds floating above us, blinking rain out of my eyes.

...

Selena made the rain spell too well. When we got back up, it was nine in the morning, and the rain seemed to want to just stay in the same place forever.

The wall surrounding the base was only broken in where Solaria had exploded. Two buildings were completely destroyed, and three were badly burned. We found David healing some people and asked him where the head of the place was.

"He's over at the wall," David said, and continued to his work. We went over there and tried to talk to some people, but they just ignored us.

"Let's go now," I muttered.

"Okay," Selena said. "Let's get our bags and find Nina and get David. I want to get out of here."

Chapter 12

We walked out and faced the jungle. A tall wall lined the border, and there was a gate that led into Yharon's territory.

"I am not looking forward to this," David muttered, and shook water off his hair.

"Then let's get it over with," I said as we walked through the gates. I turned to the visitor center and saw the tree which had captured Zach, Yohan, and Connor.

We walked along the shore to the tree, and I said, "You ready?" David took a deep breath and nodded. He drew his staff.

"I'll need your help too, Will," David said. "We need as much power as possible."

"Okay." I closed my eyes and tried to focus. The rain pounded on my head and dropped down my shoulders. I could hear every little sound.

"What do I have to do?" I asked.

"Talk to the tree."

"What?"

"Just… try."

"Okay. Uh… Hi, tree." I felt really stupid, but I guess that it was the only thing to do.

Hello, a voice said in my mind.

"Those are my friends there," I said. "Could you release them?"

No.

185

"We'll have to blast you otherwise."

Wait. I opened my eyes and saw David talking to the tree.

"Yeah," he said. "Could you release them now?" He paused and nodded.

"Thanks." The tree groaned, and I heard some muttering.

"Can't - the tree…" Zach tumbled out of the tree. He was completely covered from head to toe with vines.

"I - what?" Zach mumbled. "I was - tree, uh… Will? Selena? What am I doing here?"

"The tree got you," I explained. The tree moved again, and Yohan and Connor fell out. They also had leaves and foliage all over their bodies.

"How?" Connor said.

"I should leave now," David said.

"Ok," Selena said. "Make sure you watch us." She shook his hand.

"Bye David!" I called, and he burst into a bunch of leaves, leaving (oops! pun not intended) a scent of fresh air behind.

"He could've helped us clean up," Yohan muttered, picking grass out of his blond hair.

"Sorry," I grinned. "Do you wanna go to the visitor center? They should have some helpful stuff."

…

We learned one thing at the visitor center.

Actually, we learned a lot of things, but one important thing. Yharon's fortress was just down the river, past a functional guard tower that would shoot anyone who came within fifty yards and a grove of spiky trees that were poisonous.

Also, we learned that we should go to the waterfall for sightseeing, that the boats can leak very easily, and that we should go to the Jungle Grill for lunch.

"Well that was helpful," Selena said as we came out of the visitor center.

"There's the watchtower right there." I pointed to a tall wooden tower that had a sun guard patrolling the area.

"Well, at least we know where to go…" Yohan muttered.

"Okay!" Connor said. "Try not to die in the process!" And we started to walk toward the watchtower with a crazy sun guard on top of it.

We got across the river easily.

I flew Yohan across with Selena's help, and pretty soon, we got everyone over.

"The rain is not helping," Yohan groaned. His black eyes that used to have flames in them were now blank.

"We could summon a cloud," Selena suggested, looking at me.

"Okay." I closed my eyes and linked hands with Selena. In a few seconds, I felt the rain stop above our heads. A tiny little gray cloud hovered above us, and I commanded it to go to Yohan.

"Thanks," he said, and managed a weak smile.

"We're almost in range of the sun guard," I noted. "What should we do now?" I looked to our right, and there was a huge overhang. Below it, there was a large, churning lake.

"Let's not go down there," Zach shivered.

"The river is close to overflowing," Connor said.

"Well- whoa!" Yohan yelped. Selena fired a gust of wind at Yohan and lifted him across.

The sun guard suddenly turned and drew a bow.

"YOHAN!" I screamed. I thought that he would be dead, but the cloud surrounded him and blocked the flaming arrows.

Suddenly, the river heaved up and overflowed. I tossed Connor to the other side, hoping that he would be okay too.

"Selena," I said. "What do we do?" We walked backward as the water edged closer.

"JUMP!" she yelled.

"But I can't fly!" I complained. She grabbed me just as the water got to us, and we fell over the side of the cliff, not even sure if Nina would survive.

Did I save Selena? Sadly, no.

As we plunged to our deaths, Selena screamed, "Open your arms!" I did exactly that, and we angled into a steep glide. We still were approaching the water too fast.

Suddenly, we turned upward just as we were going to go splat on the water. We flew upward, and as we almost got to the top again, I saw that we were losing speed. I helped, but there was no way that we could reach the top of the cliff.

"Selena, c'mon," I murmured, but we lost altitude and plunged toward the water.

...

We were in some kind of underwater cave. I saw the waves sloshing around above us.

"Where… are we?" I murmured. I saw Selena already up, talking to a woman in a blue dress. Her face was pale, but I couldn't really tell.

"The eighteenth!" Selena protested. "We don't have any time left!"

"I need to talk to the boy, too," the woman said calmly. Her voice sounded like gentle waves lapping up on the beach. I knew who this person was. She was Aquaia. She wore a green silk sleeveless dress

"I'm awake!" I yawned.

"Will!" Selena said. "Oh, thank goodness you're alive! Let's hurry! It's already nine o'clock of the eighteenth!"

"What?" I gasped. "We were… what about Connor and Yohan?"

"Aquaia told them. They're fine. But hurry!"

"Okay!" I got out of the bed that I was on and walked up to her.

"I know that I've wasted your time," Aquaia said. "But, I need to tell you some important things. First, Abyssion talked to me, and I told him to not eat demigods when they enter the water. But, you'll have to build a shrine for him."

"WHAT?" Selena thundered. "He almost killed John!"

"I know and another thing that will be vital to you. Here is four hours later than Los Angeles. You have four hours extra time."

"I waited this long… FOR THIS?"

"I would expect more respect from you," Aquaia said. "But I must release you now." She waved her hand, and we floated up and out into Yharon's jungle, once again.

We collapsed on the cliffside, the rain still pouring down over our shoulders. The river still overflowed and poured into the cliff, and I grabbed Selena before she could fall back into the pit.

"Where's Yohan and Connor?" Selena grumbled. I looked around and saw the watchtower. There was no sun guard up there. Instead, I saw two people, sitting around a fire.

"Over there." I pointed to the tower.

"Really?" Selena complained. "They get a warm fire and everything, but we just get a yucky old water cave!" The water surged and knocked her down. We were already drenched, but now she was covered in mud and grime.

"Oh well," she grumbled. "Let's go."

We walked up the spiral staircase and entered the room. Instantly, Yohan had a fire dagger at my throat and Selena was tangled with vines.

"Whoa!" I said, raising my hands in surrender. "We come in peace!"

"Oh!" Yohan said, turning red. "Oops. Sorry."

"So, what happened?" Selena asked, kneeling down by the campfire.

"What happened to you?" Connor exclaimed, brushing a chunk of mud off her pants.

"Oh," Selena said, and we told them about Aquaia and what she told us about the water.

"And your story?" I asked.

"Well," Connor said. "I just blasted the guy with my powers, and he disintegrated."

"He had this really sweet knife." Yohan showed me the blade in his hand. "His spear and bow weren't here when we came up."

"Cool," Selena said, brushing her hair behind her ear.

"Should we go now?" I asked. "It's... um... late."

"Yeah!" Connor cheered. "Let's get out of here!"

…

Turns out, Aquaia wasn't really helping.

The water just kept on flowing until we were sloshing through a foot of murky liquid. Yohan just wasn't going to make it. He was so pale that he seemed almost like a ghost.

"Yohan," I said.

"Uhh…"

"You shouldn't be out here."

"I'm-" he stumbled and almost fell over. "I'm fine…" He clearly wasn't.

"Go back to the watchtower, please," I said. "You can't endure through this. Please."

"I can go," Nina suggested.

"Are you sure?" I asked.

"Yes!" she grumbled. "C'mon Mr. Yo Yo. Let's go."

"Don't call me that!" Yohan protested, punching Nina's arm. "Let's go now, okay?" They walked away, still arguing.

"Oh well," Selena sighed. "We have a spiky forest in front of us. Try not to get stabbed."

We forged ahead and ever so often, there would be a flash of lightning and the rumble of thunder.

"There are the trees," Connor pointed out.

"Oh… my," Zach said. We could see Yharon's fortress up ahead, the gates glimmering with heat. The citadel rose up behind the wall, and I could see the dome where Abaddon and Yharon had sat. But in front of the castle was a bunch of spiky trees. And I mean spiky.

The trees were a weird color, brown but with an orange tinge. The leaves had tiny blossoms growing on them. But even the flowers had razor sharp needles dripping green stuff that seemed like poison. Then, of course, there were the spikes on the trunks. They were huge, some of them even bigger than three feet.

They hung over the river and blocked that way too. The acid dripping into the water turned it green. But it seemed to be only on the surface of the water, and underneath was completely fine.

"We could swim underneath," I suggested.

"Or fly above," Selena said.

"You shouldn't waste your energy, though," Zach argued. "We need power to get the Vesuvius. And we might need wind power, so don't."

"Swim?" I looked at everyone for agreement.

"But we'll get wet," Connor protested.

"Do we look dry right now?" Selena laughed, brushing her wet, dripping hair behind her ears.

"No," Connor muttered.

"Make sure you don't touch the acid," I warned.

"I'll go scout ahead!" Zach said, and he turned into an eagle and flew off.

"Coming?" Selena called to us, and she dove into the water. I waded in too, and I was surprised at the coldness of the water.

I saw Selena almost through the river to the other side. I took a deep breath and plunged into the depths of the frigid stream.

I was doing good at first. I made it halfway through and was feeling fine. I was almost out when I felt a tug on my shoe. I turned back and saw that a vine had grabbed onto it.

I tried tugging at it, but it was no use. Then, Selena saved my life again. She came back into the water and saw me. She swam toward me and untangled my shoe from the vines. My lungs were close to bursting by then.

Finally, my head came out of the water and I breathed in the fresh, cool air. A few seconds later, Connor came out.

"Thanks, Selena," I said, hugging her. "You're the best."

"Thanks, Mumbo Jumbo," she smiled.

"You're welcome.""

"You better improve on your swimming skills." She grinned as we waded on shore. I squeezed some of the water out of my shirt, but it didn't help.

"I think that the water might protect us," Connor said. "Keep it on."

"Great," I muttered. The water on my clothes weighed me down and made me feel like a thousand pounds.

Suddenly, Zach appeared in front of me.

"Whoa!" I screamed, and fell back into the river.

"Oops!" Zach said. ""Well, Selena, you're not alone now." He looked back at me.

"Let's go!" I said. "What are we waiting for?"

...

While we were walking to Yharon's palace, Zach talked about what he did.

"I wanted to distract them," he explained. "So I made a few trees grow like crazy, and some guards headed that way. The spell was really powerful, though, so a lot of things around the area went crazy too."

"Oh," I said my voice sounding small. "A vine wrapped around my foot, and I nearly drowned in the river."

"Stop right there!" a voice demanded. I looked up and saw that we had arrived at Yharon's fortress. On a central that had the gate leading to Yharon's gardens, there was a sun guard. He had a gun pointed at Selena.

"A sniper!" Zach gasped. "There- what!"

"What's your business here?" the guard yelled.

"Um…" I said. "We're sightseeing?" I said it as if it was a question.

"Sure you are," the guard scoffed. He aimed his rifle and fired. I dove and knocked Selena to the side.

Luckily, the rain also slowed the bullet down, so instead of hitting my head, it hit Selena's arm. She cried out in pain and collapsed on the ground. I fired a blast of elemental energy and knocked the guard down.

"Selena," I whispered, and drew my spell tome, which was soaked.

"Uh…" she whispered. I looked at her arm. The bullet was lodged in there, and I chanted the healing spell over and over again. I managed to bring the bullet out, but she was still hurt badly.

"Ow, ow, ow." She squeezed my arm so tightly that it turned purple, and I spoke the healing spell once more.

"I think that I'll be okay," Selena said, rubbing her shoulder. "But I'll have to use my left hand for fighting."

"Let's go." I helped her up, and we walked through the gates of the palace. Zach and Connor were already there, but they were stuck.

"What the-" I muttered. There were two sets of gates, and the one on the back couldn't open.

"We need you to get through," Connor explained. "Well, the gates are usually held by some sun guards, but they aren't here. The only other way they can only be opened is by two demigods, a boy and a girl. One has to be an elemental, and the other can be any other person, as long as it's a demigod. You have to force it open, but it's extremely heavy, so…"

"I think we can do it, right Selena?" I looked at her.

"Yeah." We went forward.

"Now," Connor continued, just speak to it, and it'll give you a head start." I thought that I had spoken to too many weird things today, but I agreed.

"Hi door," I said. "We're gonna open this so could you-"

Good luck, a voice said in my head, and it rolled open a bit.

"Now!" I said to Selena, and we rolled under and started straining. It was so heavy that I felt like I would explode, but Zach and Connor managed to get through.

Finally, we released and came out. I was so relieved to come out that I collapsed on the floor. Selena went down next to me.

"Ow," I groaned.

"The door should lose some weight," Selena complained. After a few minutes, we got back up and faced the palace.

"We're in the palace. Ready, Airhead?" I asked her.

"Yes, Mumbo Jumbo," Selena grinned. "Let's go."

Chapter 13

The rain was actually helping now.

The flames trees and plants in the garden were now gray and withered. The palace that rose after the garden was steaming in the water, and the stones glowed a dull red.

"Wow," I murmured. "I don't think that we should go into the castle. I have a feeling that it's just as confusing as Abaddon's castle."

"Agreed," Zach said. "But it should be better than Abaddon's."

"Then how should we get up there?" I said. "We could fly."

"Don't worry," Selena grinned. "I think I might have a plan here, so sit tight for a bit."

...

Selena's idea was grappling hooks.

I first wondered how the heck she was going to make them, but then I realized that she was going up to the plants.

"What?" I wondered. Then I noticed that a type of tree had rope like leaves, with little claws at the end for perfect grappling places.

Selena placed her hand in one of the claws, and it closed on her fingers.

"Perfect," she muttered to herself. I decided to sit down for a bit while we were waiting. I saw that to our right, a chunk of the wall was blown apart, and tendrils of roots and leaves were growing and wrapping around walls in the area. A bunch of sun guards were hacking at the plants, but it was no use. It was spreading everywhere like an overgrown weed.

"Zach," I said. "That plant is doing its job." The roots wrapped around a soldier and choked him. The weeds grew around him and completely enveloped him. Soon, wood grew around the area, and I was pretty sure that whatever was inside there wasn't a sun guard.

"Thanks," he replied, and smiled at me.

"Almost done," Selena muttered, and she came out with two grappling hooks. "I need two more…" She cut off some more branches and started working.

Suddenly, a flaming arrow sailed from afar and grazed my leg.

"Ouch!" I yelped, and fell down.

"What was that?" Connor said, looking at me. Then he saw. "Oh no! Selena, hurry, we got company soon." Zach quickly spoke the healing spell, and I felt a lot better.

"Thanks!" I said, and I drew Malachite. Looking up, I saw an entire army of sun warriors charging at us. I summoned more and more projectiles.

"Whoa," Connor grinned. I felt a tingling in my back. I thought that someone was watching us.

Probably just the water or something, I thought.

Malachite wasn't going to keep the guards from stopping, though. I closed my eyes and tried to summon the water.

Suddenly, the rain surged down quicker, and it became sharp and deadly. It cut through the army but still wasn't enough. Connor and Zach started blasted the guards with green magic. A huge blast of magic fired from behind Zach and exploded into more vines. They wrapped around the warriors and tangled them. Then, they drew their bows and fired a volley of flaming arrows at us.

"Duck!" I cried, and the arrows splattered harmlessly against the ground behind us. The archers prepared another round of shots and I knew that we had to go.

"Selena, hurry!" I yelled.

"Help us make the plants grow," Connor said. I ran forward and thought of plants. The branches extended, and Selena finished her last grappling hook.

"Done!" she said, and handed the finished products to us. We shot the hooks at the palace, and we swung out of reach of the sun guards. Zach had a bit of trouble firing the hook (because he was dropping it constantly), but he made it.

Not a moment too soon. The arrows flew and zipped past us. We ended up on one of the wings of the palace. Not the dome, sadly, but at least we weren't barbecued.

The grappling hooks withered away as we reached the rooftops, so we were stuck there.

"Now what?" Connor mumbled.

"There was something that I wanted to tell you," Zach interrupted. "The Vesuvius, I did some research on it. It'll be harder to get than the Key of Nightmares."

"Understandable," I said.

"We'll need two people to do it. The two people need to put a hand on the pattern on the throne. The eye on the staff design will open up and start burning your hand. But you have to wait and keep your hand on there. Then, the staff pops out of the design and you have it."

"Who's going to do it, though?" I asked nervously, scanning my friend's faces.

"I can," Selena volunteered. "You guys are the better fighters anyway."

"I will," I said.

Are you sure, Will?" Connor fretted. "It's just-"

"I'll be fine," I said confidently, but I wasn't so sure on the inside. "We've done enough things together."

"So," Connor said, continuing what he had said earlier. "How will we get up there?"

"Now we fly," Zach said. "Or I could turn into an elephant, and then I could go up to the tower, and then-"

"Flying is fine," I laughed. "Selena, help me with Connor." Together, we made a tiny wind tornado and flew Connor up to the dome. Zach transformed into a bird and flew up with us.

"I'm pretty sure I know how this place works," I said once we reached the top. "There's a center staircase, and there are four rooms in the tower. Easy, right?"

"No," Connor grumbled.

"Okay, then!" I exclaimed. "Let's go!" And we descended into Yharon's palace.

There didn't appear to be any monsters or enemies down inside of the tower, but we didn't know which quarter of the tower contained the throne room.

"Where to go… where to go…" Zach muttered.

"Let's maybe check all of them?" Connor suggested. Suddenly, I heard faint footsteps.

"Someone's here!" I whispered urgently. "Hide." It actually sounded like a whole army marching. We ran down one corridor and dove into one of the rooms. It was an odd room, there were weapons scattered all over the area and boxes filled with arrows were lying around the area.

Sadly, the room we went in was exactly the one that the monsters wanted to go into. We heard some rattling on the door.

"Hide again!" Selena yelped. We piled boxes and boxes of swords and weapons around us, which probably wasn't the best idea, but it was all we had. A sword poked into Selena's arm, and she winced.

"You okay?" I whispered. She nodded, but I saw a good size cut on her arm. Suddenly, the doors burst open, and I heard the sun guard's march in.

"We're supposed to get some flaming arrows," one growled.

"Where they supposed to be?" another asked.

"There's a huge pile over there," the first warrior said. I had a sneaking suspicion that they were talking about the place we were hiding. I glanced at my friends and mouthed, "In three, two, one…" We burst out of the pile, and I controlled my green swords to point at the soldiers. Turns out, they weren't really just soldiers.

"Elite guards of Yharon!" Selena gasped. I launched the weapons while they were still confused, and the front row of guards disintegrated. Just then, I realized that they were actually monsters.

"Who are you?" a guard yelled.

"We have an appointment with Yharon!" I said, drawing Malachite.

"Yharon's busy right now!" another monster said. "There's a crazy tree that broke down a side of the wall! I can call him if you wan-"

"No, that's fine!" Connor shouted. He opened his hands, and roots shot out from the floor, pulling the elite guards down.

"What?" someone screamed, and hurled a spear at us. We ducked, and it shattered against the wall behind us.

"Let's get out of here before-" The floor started to tilt, and Selena slipped and started sliding toward the hole that the guards had just disappeared through.

"Selena!" I yelled, and tried to grab her hand. But it was too late. She kept on slipping until only her hands were holding onto the ledge.

The guards weren't done yet. Flaming arrows shot up through the hole, but they all missed and stuck to the ceiling like a pincushion.

"Don't move forward!" Selena cried. "The floor's too weak. It's going to collapse-" The floor crumbled, and I fell. I never realized that there would be a hall in the tower below us, but that's where the monsters fell.

I wondered if I could do something with the earth because I was an elemental. Just maybe… I focused on the ground and jerked my hand upward. A wall of rock came up from the ground and caught Selena.

"Thanks," she managed, but the earth was lowering. I forced the ground to go up higher, and I landed on the rocks too.

"How can you-" Selena wondered.

"I have no idea," I answered, and forced the rock to bring us back up to the room.

"Will!" Connor shouted. "Where did-"

"Jump!" I yelled to Selena, and we leaped onto the solid ground just as the pillar of earth sank back into the ground.

The building rumbled again, and more chunks of the floor came falling down.

"Let's go," Zach said.

"Good idea," I agreed, and we rushed out of the room.

"So, we got one fourth of the place covered," Selena said. "Now where…" We heard a roar that sounded like Yharon.

"Quick," I gulped. And of course, the other two rooms that we checked weren't the dumb throne room.

One of them was probably the treasury. There were piles of gold and many jewels scattered all over the floor.

"Not very organized, eh?" Connor said.

"Yeah," I agreed.

"Can I take some?" Zach asked, picking at the jewels.

"No!" Selena yelled. "Don't! They're cursed to demigods and people. If you take one, you'll-"

"Something bad?" Connor suggested.

"Yeah." There was another roar, time much closer.

"Next room," Zach said. "Hurry!" We rushed across the hallway to the other room.

"Hurry guys!" Selena urged. We ran across the room. This one was like a living room. There were paintings hung up around the room, and there was a rug with a table on it. Chairs were lined up around the table, and I saw that we were probably in the dining room.

We heard footsteps pounding up a corridor, and we dashed into the throne room. A blast of fire flew past us.

"Get to the throne!" Selena pulled me over to the engraving on the chair. The door exploded open. We put our hands on the carving, and the orb on the staff opened up.

I heard fighting behind us, and I turned around for a bit, which was good, because I hadn't realized yet that the engraving was drilling a red-hot laser on my wrist.

Yharon was standing there, and I couldn't tell what exactly he was wearing, because he was enveloped in flame flames. Tendrils of white flame whipped around him, and Zach and Connor were trying to fight him off.

I turned back around and suddenly felt the pain. I saw half of some kind of staff burned on my right wrist. It looked exactly like Vesuvius.

"Hold on!" Selena muttered, and I decided to turn back around. Zach and Connor didn't stand a chance. Yharon wrapped two ropes of flame around them, and they didn't burn up right away because they were still wet.

I closed my eyes and tried to focus, and suddenly, a pointy rock jutted out and smacked into Yharon. The ropes disappeared for a second, and that gave my friends a chance to attack.

Vines dropped from the ceiling, and distracted Yharon, but he just blasted them away with a sweep of his hands. He brushed Zach and Connor aside and walked to us. The engraving on my skin was almost done, and I looked at it.

"You're a hopeless case!" Yharon laughed. I forced a blast of ice at him, but he just stepped aside.

"Why try to attack me?" he asked, lashing a fiery whip at me. It smacked Selena and me, ripping our backs, but we held on. I closed my eyes and sent a ripple of elemental power at him, and he lost focus for a bit.

"I'll take care of these midgets first," Yharon said, and drew a knife. I turned back to Selena, and I saw that the laser had only done a bit of work.

"Are you okay?" I asked her.

"No... it... it hurts..." she managed.

"C'mon," I whispered. The building rumbled and tilted. I looked back for a second and saw Yharon sliding toward the open window. The throne slid too, and it seemed like our hands were connected to the throne. We were dragged along thrown against the wall. The tower cracked and broke open. The rain poured in.

"You can do it," I said to Selena, but I wasn't sure if I could handle it anymore. My hand was really burning now, and I was sure that it would be reduced to ashes soon.

"I- I can't," Selena groaned. I grabbed her hand, channeling power into her body.

"Yes you can!" I said sternly. Suddenly, something, or something's flew from the sky. It was Nina and Yohan.

"Miss someone?" Yohan grinned as he battled against Yharon. The laser finished my hand and moved on to Selena.

"AHH!" she screamed, and her nails sank into my hand. I turned and saw that they still weren't doing good.

Then, I had an even bigger surprise.

David exploded in a flash of green light and came out to battle.

"Well, I'm here now too." He ran off to Yharon. The pain was so overwhelming now that I could hardly talk.

"Will... please..." Selena groaned. The laser was half done with the engraving now, but the throne was growing dangerously bright. The tower shuddered again, and we slid way too close to the hole in the wall. The building cracked again, and part of the floor gave way. The whole side of the wall broke off, and from there, I wasn't exactly sure of what was happening.

My vision was blanking, and I saw flashes of the battle around us. Our friends were doing good, but I knew that they would be defeated soon.

I saw Yharon turn around and fire a flame blast at us. It hit the ground and exploded into a bunch of flames. They stuck into our backs like shrapnel, and I felt myself drift into a vision.

...

I was with Selena again, and I saw Fort Azari drift into view. It was raining super hard. I turned to Selena.

"You did this?" I asked in amazement.

"Yeah." The lake was flooded and the water threatened to go even higher. People were rushing around, trying to block up the water, but it was no use. Soon, Fort Azari would be flooded, and it would be our fault. I looked at Selena's wrist. The burning image of the staff was complete. The vision faded away.

...

"Ahh!" I yelled and a staff protruded from the throne and whacked my face. I grabbed it although my hand was burning.

"Selena!" I yelled, and she was lying on the floor. I hauled her to the hole in the wall, where the rain splashed through.

"I… what…?" Selena muttered.

"Guys!" I screamed through the howling air and wind. "I got it! Let's go!"

"No, you didn't!" Yharon yelled, and created a fiery shield and trapped us. I raised Vesuvius, and the tower leaned. A huge meteor smashed through the tower and hit Yharon in the face.

"Agghhh!" he screamed, and the shield fell.

"David, teleport them to Fort Azari!" I yelled. He nodded, and they zoomed away.

"Selena, I'm gonna have to trust you, okay?" I muttered to her. She was still conscious, luckily, and she could stand up. I hugged her and jumped out of the tower as it leaned and smashed into the ground, blasts from Yharon following me and hitting me. But it didn't matter. We were free. The wind caught us, and we soared into the air.

...

"Selena," I whispered.

"Uhh…"

"Are you okay?"

"I dunno… What happened? Did I have a vision… what?" I told her of all that had happened.

"Okay…" Fort Azari floated into view. The moon was just reaching its peak. The rain was still pounding, but the moon made a clear circle of light around the darkness.

"We're back," I whispered to Selena.

Chapter 14

We crash landed in the lake.

I wished for a graceful landing, but we created quite an explosion because we were carrying two of the most powerful weapons in the world, right?

We swam (or rather, I swam) out of the lake and we immediately passed out on the grass.

When we woke, the rain had cleared, but it was a foggy morning.

"We have to report to Abaddon!" I suddenly gasped. "Selena, let's go. Come on!" With my help, we dragged ourselves into the Meeting House.

"Abaddon," I said, and he looked up from his chains.

"Yes? I see that you have retrieved the Vesuvius. I guess that I'll have to withdraw the Corruption now. Oh well." Randy came out from a room in the Meeting House.

"What will we" he was muttering to himself, but he paled when he saw us. "Will and Selena! You're back!"

"Bring me out to fix the Corruption," Abaddon demanded. "And don't worry. I'm on your side now. Release my chains." We did as he told, and we went out to the borders of Fort Azari. The Corruption had spread to almost the walls of Fort Azari.

Abaddon raised his hands and closed his eyes. The corroded grass turned to green. The flaking boulders turned back to normal. The trees up righted.

"Wow," I murmured. Suddenly, the fog turned yellow. At first, I thought that it was Yharon or someone bad, but then I realized that it was the sun.

The mist cleared away, revealing a rolling landscape of grass and beautiful trees. A few mountains loomed in the distance as clouds drifted across the lands. Selena grasped my hand.

"Wow," she gasped.

"Yeah," I agreed. "Really wow."

…

You know what really ruined the awesome view? It started raining again. Again.

"Selena!" I complained. "What in the world is with the stupid weather?" A gust of wind blew me over onto the mushy ground.

"Wow," she said, trying to pick herself off the ground. "We should go to the infirmary now." So we did. Connor, Zach, Yohan, and Nina were already in there.

"Hi," Yohan grinned. "Fell in the mud again?"

"Courtesy of Aer," I muttered.

In a while, we were a bit better, and Selena could actually stand without my help.

It was time for dinner, so we headed into the living room of the Meeting House. We got our dinner and found Zach waiting for us at the lake. It wasn't raining anymore, and the air smelled fresh and clean.

"Zach!" I cried, and I ran toward him.

"Hey guys," he said. "It's nice to not worry a bit." We sat down next to him.

"Are you feeling okay?" I asked him.

"I'm fine," he answered. "But - wait. What happened to your hand?" I looked down at the marks of the gray rod and red orb on my right wrist.

"Vesuvius," I muttered.

"But, I never knew that it would do that to you."

"We've pretty been branded for stealing one of the world's most powerful weapons," Selena sighed. She grabbed my hand, examining the marks.

"Oh well," I said. After that, we didn't say a word as we watched the sun slowly sink to the horizon.

"Will!" I heard Randy call. "I wanted to talk to you."

"Okay," I answered.

"About Vesuvius, I first wanted to tell you all that you did a good job. But, I want to say a few things. Selena, you too, because you got brand"

"Will it be there forever?" I interrupted.

"Sadly, yes," Randy answered. "It makes monsters want to go after you even more, and also about Vesuvius. If it breaks, it releases a surge of energy just like Malachite does, but we still have to use it. Selena, come with me."

"Can we go too?" I asked.

"Okay." We followed him back to the Meeting House. Hung up on a rack in the weapon room was the staff itself.

"Selena," Randy said. "We have all agreed to give you the Vesuvius." Selena paled.

"Really?" she muttered. "What if I lose it, or"

"The Aphelists made a magical pouch for it, so it will fit in your pocket. It is impossible to lose. As for breaking it, there is no solution for that." Randy grabbed the staff and handed it to Selena.

"Thank you," she managed. "It's- it's a big honor, I guess." Randy gave her the pouch, and Vesuvius shrank instantly as she put it in there.

"You can go back now," Randy said, and we walked back out to the lake.

"I don't know," Selena murmured. "I'm kinda scared."

"You'll be fine," I laughed, patting her back. "We've already survived too much. Don't worry." We sat back down and finished our dinners. The sun was about to go down, but we could still stay at the lake.

While we were away, the demigods had set up a bunch of lamps, and there were now pathways connecting to the different cabins. Just as the sun sank below the horizon, the lights instantly blazed on. They weren't like regular lights. They were balls of flame, glowing in the darkness.

As night fell, a thick fog swirled around the area, and the land seemed kind of mysterious, the only light source dampened by the mist.

"Can you summon a flame?" Selena whispered to me.

"Sure." I opened my hand, and a ball of flame formed. I willed it to hover above us, and soon it was casting a big circle of light around us. Other demigods still also were outside, chatting, and I finally felt like I was just a normal person, sitting with my friends while a magical ball of light burned above us.

"We still didn't have the sniper battles," Selena complained. "Will, you've missed way too much."

"It's fine. Besides, I've had fun not dying on the quests, so I don't think that I've missed too much."

"We'll have our battles tomorrow," a voice said behind us. I turned and saw that it was Randy again. "You'll finally get to enjoy Fort Azari."

...

The next day felt too normal. Other than the fact that people kept on staring at me, probably because of that annoying brand on wrist, we had a fine day. Some of the classes were boring, of course, but that wouldn't stop me from enjoying it.

Time and time again, the marks on my wrist kept on hurting, and I saw that Selena was experiencing the same thing.

"You okay?" she asked me. I gritted my teeth but still answered, "Yeah, I'm fine."

After dinner, we gathered up and prepared all our weapons of the sniper battles.

"Who am I going with?" I said.

"Me, dummy," Selena answered, punching my arm.

"Ouch," I grinned.

"Everyone ready?" Randy called. We all cheered.

"Okay. Let's head over to the mountains now. You know the rules. Pairs of two. Only steal the other team's rock, nothing else. Also, there are only four groups today, as some people didn't want to join. Good luck everybody!"

...

We stopped behind a clump of boulders that surrounded us on every side. I heard some cracking from behind us, and I turned. It was some kind of monster that brandished two swords.

"Monster!" I reported and fired an arrow at it. The monster crossed its two blades and deflected the arrow. It flew off into the distance.

"What are you doing?" Selena growled.

"I dunno." Selena launched another arrow at the monster and caught it in the face. The monster crumbled to dust.

"What kind of monster was that?" I whispered.

"Have you been listening, Mumbo Jumbo? That's a Selenian." I saw a flash of blue in the distance.

"Selena! Cryonites."

"What? Where?" An arrow whizzed past our heads. Selena notched an arrow that would detect the other team's stone and bring it back to us.

"Ahh!" I heard some yelling, and a stone came back to us.

"Nice," Selena said.

"I think that was Nina," I said. "She's probably weaker in the volcano area-" An arrow smacked into the stones, and they scattered.

"Where'd they go?" We crawled the area, searching for the stones. We found one, but the other fell in an open area.

"Here, Selena," I said, giving the stone to her. "I'm going to run for it."

"Will, don't-" But I was already gone. I got to the stone, okay but a net fell on me right away.

"Some help here?" I groaned as I struggled to get up. Two figures approached, and I saw that it was Yohan and another Aphelist.

"Sorry, Will," Yohan grinned, but another arrow bounced off his armor and knocked him aside. I hoped that it was Selena, but two other people stood on the mountain. I had no idea who they were, but one reached out his hand, and the stone came flying to him. The Aphelists were out of the game.

"Selena," I called. Then I saw where she was. She flew from the sky and crashed onto the people on the peak, stealing their gems.

We had won, although I was stuck under a super heavy net.

"Selena!" I shouted.

"What?"

"I'm sort of stuck, so could you help me?"

"No."

"Okay," I laughed. "Thanks for helping out." Selena flew down, and we untangled me from the net.

"Let's go down now," Selena said, and together, we flew back down to the Meeting House.

There was a bunch of cheering (plus a bunch of booing) when we arrived at the Meeting House. We had to go to sleep right away after that, which was sort of sad, but it was a good day.

...

I had a nice dreamless sleep, but was waken up by some pounding on my door.

"What is it?" I yawned.

"It's me!"

"Selena?"

"Yeah. The gods want to see you. You know that there's a yearly meeting they have. This time, it'll be at Aer's palace. They've invited us to come, so get up now."

"But I just was having a good nap!"

"Will!"

"Okay," I muttered, and I quickly dressed and went outside. It was still foggy from last night, and Selena looked kind of scary in the mist.

"Let's go!" she said. She was wearing a thick coat around her, and I realized that it was actually really cold.

"I need a jacket," I complained. "But I don't have one."

"Here!" She brought out a white jacket from her coat.

"Where in the world did you get that-?"

"Aer gives me things sometimes. Now let's go!" Selena answered quickly, and we rushed off.

"How do we get there?" I asked nervously.

"Taxi." Selena snapped her fingers, and there was an explosion of clouds in front of us. A white taxi was in front of us.

"What?" I said. "Who's driving this?"

"No one!" Selena answered. "You just gotta hope for the best."

"Umm…"

"C'mon, Will." She grabbed my hand and dragged me into the shotgun seat. Selena sat down on the driver's seat.

"You're… driving?" I said.

"No," she answered. "I'm just sitting here-" The car suddenly jolted and started flying forward at a scary speed.

"Oh, gosh," I muttered, and this time it was my hand who grabbed Selena. The fog turned into clouds until we burst into the air. We flew so fast that even Selena looked a bit nervous.

"AHHHHHH!" we screamed. (It might still be just me, but who cares, still?) I saw Aer's palace up ahead.

"What do we do?" I yelled. "We're going to crash!"

"Eject!" Selena threw open her door and jumped.

"What?" I screamed, and did the same. The wind caught me, and I soared into the air. I saw Selena up ahead, her brown hair flying backwards. I caught up with her, and we soared down into the courtyard.

Many demigods were already there. I spotted Zach, Sarah, who I realized was with Yohan on the mountain, Yohan, Nina, and others.

As we descended, I had a proper look at the fortress. There was a white wall that surrounded the whole area, and there were many fountains and a lake in the courtyard. The whole place was filled with green grass, and there were dirt pathways leading everywhere.

Then, of course, there was the castle. It sat next to the lake, and was absolutely huge. It was made of white brick like the rest of the palace, and was five stories tall. The bottom floor was completely open air, and there were many large thrones situated in a semicircle. The rest of the floors had windows, and I couldn't see into them.

We landed gracefully, and I suddenly spotted someone.

"Cryos is here?" I gasped.

"She is the goddess of snow. You know… the Cryonites?" Selena answered.

"Wait," I said. "We really knocked her off of a cliff?"

"Yeah," I spotted gods walking around the gardens. I spotted Aer talking to someone else, a bright orange person who looked sort of like Yharon. Then I realized that he was Aphelion. Abaddon was standing right next to him, so I figured that they were going to work together. I saw Aquaia talking with Cryos, and she shot a smile at us. Cryos turned for a moment and froze us for a moment with a glare. Literally froze.

"Gosh," I shivered. "There's no need…"

"Yeah," Selena muttered. We went to try to find our friends, but I suddenly froze in my tracks. I saw Reality talking to another man who looked suspiciously like me. He had black hair and the same face as me, but he otherwise was completely different. At first, he seemed just like a regular man wearing a suit and tie, but he glowed an aura of elemental power. He seemed so powerful and strong. I was sure that he was Galaxius.

He turned to face me and called, "William!"

"Dad?" I said quietly. I walked toward him with Selena following close behind.

"Yes," he said. "I am your dad. I've been watching throughout these years, and I'm proud of everything you've done." He held out his hands, and I hugged him. It felt awkward doing it, but it felt right.

"Good job, Will," he murmured softly. I felt tears come to my eyes, but I forced them down.

"Will!" I heard Zach call.

"But you should go off to your friends," he gave me one last smile and turned away. I felt weird. I had just met my dad for the very first time.

"Will!" Zach yelled and ran to me. He gave me a funny look. "You okay? You look... odd." I nodded and took a quick swipe at my eyes.

"How'd you get up here?" I finally asked.

"Abaddon teleported us. What about you?"

"Well," I said, looking at Selena. "We got an air taxi and flew up here. It was not fun."

"Not my fault!" Selena grinned.

"Sure." There was the sound of a trumpet, and we all headed into Aer's palace. There were eight thrones in total, one of them empty. In the middle, there were two thrones for Galaxius and Reality, one of the green blue and studded with malachite crystals like the ones in the hole in front of the Cryonite's cabin.

To the right, there were the thrones of the goddesses. Aquaia's throne was first, and it didn't even look like sit table. It seemed to be made of swirling water. Next to that was Aer's throne. That didn't look like sit table either. There was just a spinning tornado of air. The last one on the right side was Cryos's throne. It was an icy blue,and frozen crystals gleamed on it.

Then, on the left were the god's thrones. Aphelion sat on an orange throne that was on fire. Right next to him, Abaddon stood. Although a god, he didn't have a throne currently. Alluvion sat on a misty chair next to him.

In the center of the semicircle, there was a cushion that was woven of leaves and twigs. It was probably an honorary seat for the Grovites, who didn't really have a god who could sit in a seat.

"What are they going to do?" I asked nervously to Selena. All the gods and goddesses gathered in one room sort of scared me.

"Will Hanson, Selena Mayne, please come up," Aer called.

"Let's blast them!" Cryos announced immediately. "They attacked me."

"Only because you tried to kill us first," Selena muttered. The Cryonites behind us grumbled in agreement.

"He is my son," Galaxius argued. "I will not have him blasted."

"Just a little bit?" Cryos pleaded. She drew a frozen knife and started cleaning it with a towel.

"No," Aer said. "My daughter will be left alone."

"Why?" Cryos complained. She tried to stand up, but Aquaia just sighed and splashed Cryos's face with water.

"Are you awake?" Aquaia said.

"No," Selena muttered.

"I heard that!" Cryos snapped.

"All in favor in not blasting them?" Galaxius asked. Most of the gods and goddesses voted to not blast us. Cryos insisted to blast us. Abaddon abstained, but we didn't get blasted, so I took that as a good sign.

"We owe a lot for getting Abaddon-" Reality said.

"Thanks a whole ton," Abaddon muttered.

"And for retrieving Vesuvius from Yharon's palace."

"What do you mean by retrieved?" I asked.

"We once had Vesuvius in our possession," Reality explained. "But we once sent some demigods on a quest"

"And they lost it," Cryos interrupted. "Because they're clumsy, and blah, blah, blah."

"Excuse me," Galaxius said. "Reality is talking."

"Oh! Well, I'm so sorry Reality," Cryos groaned. "I'll make it up for you and everything-" Alluvion waved his hand, and a rope wrapped around Cryos's mouth.

"Mmm!" she tried to say.

"As I was saying," Reality continued. "We lost Vesuvius, but your help getting it back-"

"But Yohan and Connor and Nina helped too!" I suddenly exclaimed, and then turned red. "Sorry Lord."

"Do not worry," Reality said. "But we could give you a gift."

"Not a thing," I said. "We're fine." I looked at Selena, and she nodded.

"Okay then." He sent us back to our places. The gods then talked about other problems, like setting up more bases to guard Yharon's palace, and other boring things.

After a while, the meeting was over, so we went with our friends to the lake to watch the sunset.

"When are we going to leave here?" I asked Selena.

"Well, we could just relax here for a bit, but we'll go back pretty late," she answered.

"Will we take a taxi again?" I joked.

"Yeah."

"Seriously?" I groaned. Later, we had dinner, and it was better than anything at Fort Azari. I had my favorite food, sushi, and thanks to Alluvion, he made a thick mist flow through the whole palace and made us lose track of where we were going.

Finally, we had to leave. Selena and I wanted to go earlier than everyone else, so we went outside of the walls.

"What do we do?" I asked her.

"Jump!" Selena said, and she ran off the edge, pulling me with her.

Chapter 15

I will not recommend jumping off of a floating island if you are scared of heights and also value your life.

I, luckily, did not care much of both those things, so I was fine.

We soared into the clouds, and when we came out of them, I saw Fort Azari in the distance. Alluvion decided to be nice enough to put a thick haze of fog around the area, so the whole place seemed mysterious and deserted. I saw some demigods walking around already, and they waved at us as we flew by them.

"Where do you want to go?" I asked her as the wind whipped in our faces.

"I don't know," she answered. "Wherever you want to go," So we just flew around the place, looking at the cabins in the moonlight.

"Can we go to the front?" I said. We soared to where I originally flew in a car propelled by some storm weavers.

"Race you to the mountain!" Selena yelled, and she flew off.

...

We spent the rest of the night flying around and talking like two normal human beings. It was really fun, so you should definitely try it out.

Finally, at dawn, we came back down. Yohan was sitting at the lake, and we went over to him.

"Nice flying tricks," he said. "I was watching you guys the whole time." As I got closer to him, I felt the brand on my arm burning. I turned to Selena and saw that her's was glowing a dim red.

"What the-" I muttered.

"It's me," Yohan sighed. "Because I'm an Aphelist, I'm sort of connected to Yharon. Your brand will burn much more if you get close to Yharon." We sat down next to him, and I dipped my hands in the cool water. The burning sensation seemed to go away. Selena did the same, and I watched the glow fade away.

Selena grabbed my hand and looked at the markings. "Yours is different than mine," she suddenly pointed out.

"What?" I said. I looked at her wrist and saw that Vesuvius wasn't on it. Instead, there was Yharon's mark that I saw on the banners in the dream I had so long ago.

"Yharon's insignia," Yohan muttered.

"What's that?" I asked him.

"When Yharon was a soldier under Oblivion, he had that badge. Do you know about the story?"

"No."

"Okay. Well, Oblivion was the father of all the gods and goddesses. Right as they were born, Oblivion wanted to make them come to his side right away. But some didn't. So those were the good gods. Oblivion tried to defeat them. But he lost. Also, Oblivion made monsters. When Oblivion came, monsters formed. So after Oblivion lost, Yharon wanted to become king."

"But how did Oblivion get in a box?"

"Yharon trapped him in there. But he still wants to overthrow the gods. So he plans to unleash Oblivion."

"Well, he doesn't have the key anymore, or the box."

"The chest is in his fortress," Yohan said.

"But we knocked down his tower. Wouldn't that destroy"

"We don't know where the chest is," Selena said. "Anyways, the chest wouldn't break that easily."

"I wish it could," I muttered.

"He can reforge it," Selena said. "But only with an Eternal Flame and the only one that exists is right there." She pointed to the ball of flame on the tower.

Suddenly, Yohan's eyes closed.

"Wha-" Selena tried to keep awake, and she got up and stumbled. I stood up too.

"Selena!" I said, and she leaned on me. "What are you..." Then my eyelids felt heavy, and I tried hard to keep awake.

C'mon, Selena." I glimpsed a shadow on the walls of Fort Azari.

"Uhhh..." Selena groaned.

"Selena!" I yelled, also to myself, and we became fully conscious again. Selena's eyes fluttered open.

"Someone!" I said, taking a deep breath. "Is on the-" But Selena could think faster than me, even when fast asleep. She flew off, and I went after her.

I spotted a flaming girl holding the Eternal Flame, Solaria.

"You will not defeat me again!" she snarled, and waved her hand. A wall of fire exploded in front of us, so we flew over it. I blasted her with ice, but she summoned a lava shield around her.

"You won't get away!" I screamed, and flew straight to her.

The good news: I shattered her shield. The bad news: my head hurt like crazy. Selena took the opportunity to charge Solaria, but she blasted her with flames, and she fell down next to me.

"I'm sorry," Solaria said. "I should kill you, but I want to see you try to defeat Yharon. Good bye." She exploded into flames, and we were thrown off the wall and onto the ground. The tower groaned as flames and hot shrapnel pelted our faces. The wall started leaning, and I lost consciousness.

…

I woke up still lying on the ground. It was morning. I tried to move, but I saw that my legs were pinned down.

"Selena?" I groaned.

"Uh…" she said. "What… what happened?"

"Solaria," I answered. "She… she… stole…" I was too tired to talk anymore. I heard footsteps behind us.

"Will!" Randy yelled. "Selena! What…" He paused as he looked at the wreckage in front of him.

"I-" I croaked, and passed out again.

…

When I woke, I was in the infirmary. Selena was in bed next to me, and she was awake too.

"Selena?" I said. "Are you okay?"

"Yeah…" She tried to sit up but immediately fell back down.

"Solaria stole the Eternal Flame!" I said. "We have to…" Someone stepped into the room.

"You won't be going anywhere in your state."

"Randy?" I groaned.

"Yes. Although they have the Eternal Flame, it will take a while to forge the key again."

"But-"

"No." Randy's tone was so stern that I knew that it would be impossible convincing him.

"Okay, but… but..."

"Do you know how long it took to forge the Key of Nightmares?" Randy asked me.

"No…"

"It took one century-"

"What? But Oblivion will never be released-"

"Without the Eternal Flame. With it, it most likely would take one year or so."

"So send someone now!" Selena spoke up. She was so quiet for the moment that I forgot that she was there.

"You've had an exciting summer already," Randy said. "You need to rest for now."

"But-" He waved his hand in the air, and I fell back asleep.

...

For the first time in a long time, dreams found me. Thanks, Alluvion!

I saw Solaria in Yharon's palace, holding the Eternal Flame.

"I got it," she said.

"My daughter," Yharon murmured.

Daughter? I thought. Then, everything fit. That made sense. Suddenly, Yharon tensed, and grinned.

"It does make sense," he said, and turned to stare directly at me. "Alluvion, my disrespectful brother, always butting in on my conversation" He shot a solar flare straight at me, and I my dream shattered.

…

I woke up with a start. My hair was smoking. My eyebrows were singed.

"What the…" I muttered.

"Did you have a dream?" Selena asked me. She was still lying down, but she was awake.

"Yeah."

"You can get hurt in dreams too. Alluvion should be careful about what he's doing."

"Wait… what? Really?"

"Yes. It's definitely possible."

"Then, how…"

"It's dangerous," Selena said. "I don't think that any demigod has died from it, but it's still really deadly. It's where you get pulled too far into the dream, and you actually live in it. It's scary."

"Can you get up now?" I asked her.

"Maybe… we fell from a tower, okay? Don't expect too much from us!" She tried to get up, but stumbled and crashed landed on my bed.

"Good job," I laughed. I also tried to stand up, and with Selena's help, we could both walk.

We limped outside of the Meeting House. It was the day, maybe seven in the morning, but (of course) it was foggy and rainy.

"Great weather," Selena muttered. Someone came out of the fog. His black eyes were filled with fire.

"Yohan!" I called. When he came close, my hand started smoking.

"Hi, guys. I haven't seen you in a long time. Where were you…" He frowned, trying to remember what happened.

"We were-"

"Yeah. We were talking, and then I fell asleep…" Suddenly, the fog turned yellow and golden and brilliant, and then cleared.

"Over there," Selena pointed.

"Oh…" I told him of everything that had happened.

"Why don't we go down to the lake…" Selena suggested. We agreed and walked down. I dipped my hand in the water, and the burning died down.

"I won't be able to stay out here for long," Yohan sighed. "This weather isn't going to help."

"You should go in," I said, and patted his back. He walked off to the mountain.

"We'll be fine, for now," I said. "Randy said, you know?"

"I guess," Selena muttered. "Will, you know, I'll be going to my dad in the school year."

"Really?"

"I promised him… but I'm still not sure."

"You'll be fine, Selena," I promised. We sat there for the rest of the morning, watching the sun rise.

Later, we went off to our classes. It felt like a normal day with my friends. We had dinner, and I wanted to go to sleep early because of my wounds. Before I could go back to my cabin, Randy grabbed me.

"Sorry, but you have to go to the infirmary," he said firmly.

"But-" He grabbed me and pulled me into the Meeting House.

"You have to heal completely before you can do anything, Will," he said. "You know that you broke both legs and your left arm? The healing hasn't completely healed you yet."

"Okay." Selena was already in the room, sitting upright on a bed. She smiled at me when I came in.

"Hey Mumbo Jumbo," she grinned. "You are walking without me now?"

"Yeah."

"Well, let's go to sleep now." I got into another bed and Selena turned off the lights.

"Good night," I said, and I fell into a dreamless sleep.

…

The next days of summer were normal. I completely healed from my injuries, so I could do all my activities again.

Then came the last day of summer, where I had to decide if I wanted to stay at camp or go back home.

I thought about it while I was sitting in my cabin. I gazed around at the plain furniture and bunk bed that I was sitting on. It was really fun and nice here, not having to worry about being eaten by monsters every five seconds. But then, I would have to think about my mom. A whole year living with her? I really didn't know. Just then, someone knocked on the door.

"Come in!" I said. The door creaked open, and Selena stepped in. I waved her over, and she sat on the bed next to me.

"So," I asked. "Are you staying here, or are you heading out?"

"I'm going to go with my dad to New York City. It'll be safe there, since Abaddon's on our side now. I'll be going to a public school, so I'll blend in, and hopefully no monsters we see me. What about you?"

"I haven't decided yet. I wanted to go to Randy to ask him."

"Okay then. I'll see you soon." She left the room, and I went to Randy to ask him.

"It would be better for you stay here," he said.

"But the apartment is pretty close," I argued. "And I think I can defend myself, maybe."

"Just maybe."

"Yeah."

"I guess you could. I'm fine with that. But you'll attract a lot of monsters. Just be careful." Suddenly, I had a question.

"Won't Selena be really far away, though, in New York?" I asked.

"She will, but we only have the sun monsters to deal with, and the Oblivion monsters, but New York City is Abaddon's territory. She'll be fine."

"Can you contact my mom now?"

"Sure," Randy answered. "You should go now. I'll see you later."

"Bye!" I called, and ran off to the lake to have one last look at it before I left. I found Selena already there, talking to Zach.

"Hi, guys!" I yelled.

"Hey!" Zach said. "We were just about to go find you."

"Oh! Zach, where will you go?" I asked, sitting down next to them.

"I'm going home too," Zach answered. "My mom and dad also are in Los Angeles, pretty close to your apartment. Hey just moved there from another location because they found some better job for biology, and this location is closer. I want to convince them to go to the same school you're going to. Speaking of which, where are you going?"

"Probably some private school, and not the same one as last year. They kicked me out, you know."

"Oh yeah," Selena added. "I'll be going to Los Angeles, too. My dad is a lawyer for some guy in Los Angeles, so I'll be coming over during winter break."

"Oh no…" I grinned. "I'll never get rid of her, will I?"

"No, you won't," Selena answered. "Oh! My dad's here. I gotta go!"

"My mom's here too!" Zach said. "Will, I think that Randy told me that you're coming with me. Let's go."

"Talk to me if you can," I told her, and hugged her. I would be missing her for a while.

"Don't get eaten by monsters," she said.

"Great advice from Airhead."

"Race you to the car!" she yelled, and started sprinting to the entrance of Fort Azari.

"I'll miss you too," I whispered to all the buildings around me, and then got up and flew after Selena.

The end

Proof

Made in the USA
Columbia, SC
12 December 2017